CAUGHT

CAUGHT

BOOK TWO
OF THE
NAUTILUS LEGENDS

EMMA SHELFORD

This is a work of fiction. Names, characters, places, and incidents either are the product of the author's imagination or are used factitiously, and any resemblance to any persons, living or dead, business establishments, events, or locales is entirely coincidental.

CAUGHT

All rights reserved.

Kinglet Books
Victoria BC, Canada

Copyright © 2019 Emma Shelford
Cover design by Christien Gilston

ISBN: 978-1999101985

No part of this book may be used or reproduced in any manner whatsoever without written permission from the author except in the case of brief quotations embodied in critical articles or reviews.

www.emmashelford.com

First edition: September 2019

DEDICATION

*To the discarded name choices for my son, providing
inspiration for heroes and villains alike.*

MILES

Miles Callahan leaned back in his ergonomic office chair and put his hands behind his head to rest against the soft leather. He swiveled to take in the view. It was a glorious day, with afternoon sun sparkling off the ocean that swept in a glittering arc around Vancouver. He had paid a premium for the top floor of this office building, with nearly uninterrupted vistas of mountain and sea across a plethora of high-rises in the downtown core. Being one of the richest young entrepreneurs in the city had its privileges.

"I hear you," he said into his hands-free headset. "You know what, let's do lunch this week to hash it out, face to face. Do you like the Black Fig? My treat." He waited for confirmation, then said, "Perfect, my assistant will be in touch. You have yourself a great day."

He hung up and continued to soak up the view. He had plenty to do—the requests for his input and presence were nonstop—but what was the point in having enough money to buy this panorama if he couldn't enjoy it every now and again? His futurist tech magazine *Tomorrow*, while obviously needing his creative input, could manage itself for a few minutes.

Only a few minutes, though. The magazine was his pet project. He adored everything cutting-edge, and being the first to announce it? Well, that was the icing on the cake. And what a sweet cake it was.

"Mr. Callahan?" The soft voice of his assistant wriggled into his reverie. "Anthony Morgenstern is here to see you. Do you have time before your one o'clock meeting?"

"Send him in, Paula." He brought his body to an upright position and turned around to smile at his assistant. "That would be great."

Paula smiled back, and her silky auburn hair swished around

her shoulders when she left. She returned shortly, a middle-aged man following in her wake. He had salt-and-pepper hair above a slump-shouldered paunch, but the eyes in his careworn face were sharp and interested.

"Anthony." Miles rose to greet the man and walked around his desk with his hand outstretched. "Good to see you. Please, sit down."

Miles motioned toward two club chairs covered in smooth leather ideally positioned to enjoy the view. He preferred to hold meetings in these chairs. It was much less formal than looming over a desk at visitors like a stern headmaster with a wayward student. There was a time for the desk, of course, but people responded better to the personal touch. Miles hadn't climbed so far by being a slouch at reading other people.

"Hello, Miles." Anthony sat heavily. "I'm in Vancouver for a conference this week. I had a few hours before my flight back. Thanks for making the time."

"I'm glad you thought of me. You know I always have time for you. How are Linda and the kids?"

Anthony was not a friend—Miles had very few people in his life who had earned that title, and even fewer he truly trusted—but he was an excellent contact. As director of the Vancouver Island Health Authority, he oversaw all hospitals on the island. It seemed tangential to Miles' interests, but he had learned over the years that no contact was a poor contact. Everyone was useful, somehow.

However, there was no point in having a contact who wasn't loyal or who didn't share interesting tidbits, so Miles made sure to ramp up the friendliness with his contacts. A large donation to one of Anthony's new hospitals had sweetened Anthony's opinion of him, and he now kept his ears open for noteworthy news aligned to Miles' interests.

Predictably, Anthony smiled at Miles' personable question.

"Great, thanks for asking. Molly's been accepted to the University of Toronto for September, and she's very excited."

"I'll put in a good word for her with the dean," Miles said. "He's an old fishing buddy. What can I do for you today?"

Anthony settled more comfortably in his chair.

"There's a rumor going around."

"I'm listening."

"There were a couple of cases mid-island of a bad reaction to some new drug. Only a few cases, mind you, but we're always on the alert when new drugs are involved. My people hunted around and found the name of the producer." Anthony reached into his pocket and extracted a slip of paper with a name on it. He handed it to Miles. "These are only rumors, you understand. It's difficult to prosecute, since this product isn't a banned substance yet, and we can't definitively prove that it was this drug that caused the reaction."

"What's your next step?" said Miles. He wasn't sure where Anthony was going with this, but he must have a point if he had bothered to come to Miles' office.

"Wait, there's more. The cases were minimal and isolated, and beyond keeping tabs, there isn't a lot we can do. But the rumor-mill churned out more: if the drug is used in a certain way—underwater, apparently—there is an enhancing effect."

"What kind of enhancement?" Miles said. He leaned forward in his interest. This was what he lived for. This was why he treated his contacts so well, because once in a long while, they delivered exactly what he wanted to hear. People on the ground were worth their weight in gold, and Anthony was no pixie.

"Speed and strength, I believe." Anthony looked concerned. "It seemed like your kind of thing. What's more, if someone like you got it handled by a proper entity, we could get it off the street, controlled. I don't like the thought of unregulated drugs floating around."

"Absolutely," Miles said. "There are enough of those without adding to the mix. And why are these people needing the hospital? Clearly, there are contamination issues. I'll certainly have my people check into it. For safety reasons, we need this off the underground market.”

“I knew you were the right person to talk to about this,” said Anthony, rising. “I’ll leave it in your capable hands. I’d better push off—I’m sure you have things to do—but thanks for listening.”

“Of course.” Miles stood and shook Anthony’s hand firmly. “Any time. Say hello to Linda for me, will you? And tell her I had quiche at Chez Pierre the other night, and it didn’t hold a candle to hers.”

Once Anthony had taken his leave, Miles poked his head out of the door.

“Paula? Send for Tangled Net, please.”

He retreated to his office and looked at the view, his hands behind his back and his mind whirling with possibilities.

A minute later, two men appeared, wearing suits. One was tall with a bland expression, and the other was shorter with copious muscles under his suit jacket.

“Hello Gavin, Flint. I’m glad they sent you two. I have an assignment for you.” He handed the taller Gavin the slip of paper. “Find this man. I need to know what he knows about a drug he produces. It causes hallucinations above water and enhances strength and speed underwater.”

“How would you like us to get the information?” the stockier Flint asked. Miles smiled.

“However you can.”

CORRIE

It had taken a week and a half, but Corrie Duval had finally managed to isolate a protein. It was from a slime sample of the unicorn fish that she and Zeb had captured on his boat, the *Clicker*. It was not an easy method, involving many steps and numerous chemicals and pieces of equipment, some of which she'd had to borrow from other labs on the sly. She'd had to work evenings, when her lab mates weren't around, to avoid awkward questions.

But she finally had an isolated protein sample. It didn't tell her anything by itself, of course, but it was necessary to learn more about the slime and its effects. Now, she finally had something to play with.

Corrie jiggled her leg in excitement as she prepared a small portion of her isolated protein for the mass spectrometer at her tidy lab bench. She would finally get some data from this sample. It was tough, working for so many days with no results. Her careful prep work would hopefully show something. She wasn't sure what, but she was excited, nonetheless. She didn't even know what to hypothesize, except that whatever she found would be strange. Strange was only to be expected with the unicorn fish.

She was pipetting reagents into tubes when she heard a voice.

"Hey, Corrie," her lab mate Daniel said. He peered over her shoulder at her lab bench. "What are you working on?"

Corrie froze then forced herself to relax. It wasn't like the chemicals screamed "Unicorn fish alert! A weirdo works here!" She had thought that Daniel wouldn't arrive until later in the morning, but she could deflect questions easily enough.

"Mass spec prep," she said quickly. "There's so much to do after my cruise. I want to wrap up as much as possible before I go out again next week."

Daniel nodded.

"Fair enough. No point in going if your sampling method is crap. Don't want to repeat something that doesn't work." He picked up a reagent bottle and looked at the label. "What are you running through the mass spec?"

"I want to get a protein signature for my metabolites," she said. "This is a test run, to make sure my methods are tight. Proof of concept, right? I don't want to waste samples perfecting my technique."

"Good idea." Daniel pushed off from the bench. "Just don't test too much. Get some real data, too. You can get paralyzed by too much testing."

After he walked away, Corrie let out her breath with relief. Little did Daniel know; she wasn't testing at all. It was her first time preparing mass spectrometry samples, and the unicorn fish was the guinea-pig. She hoped she knew what she was doing. She really wanted results.

By the time she had loaded the mass spectrometer and it had finally run through its cycles, it was almost lunchtime. Corrie's stomach was growling, but she opened the data output on the computer and had a quick look.

The protein was almost entirely composed of one amino acid. While that was strange enough, the readout showed that this amino acid was slightly different from any other amino acid known to science. Was the machine not working properly? The control looked fine. Why would the amino acid of this protein be different? Amino acids were the fundamental building blocks of life. There were only twenty-two of them, and they were like the letters of the alphabet. Proteins could be composed of many different amino acids, like words and sentences, but the alphabet that made up those words didn't change.

Corrie wondered where to go from here. Knowing the chemical composition of the protein was good and necessary, but it didn't tell her anything about function. She shelved the strange amino acid signature to ponder another day. It would be amazing if she could test the isolated protein to see whether it was the compound that produced hallucinations, but there were so many hoops to jump through, ethics boards and funding and what not, that it was an impossibility.

Maybe it would be possible if she were privately backed by a donor. She wondered again about Zeb's financial state. He was still out there, driving around the *Clicker* for fun, and he had invited her for another week of sampling. Although he didn't look rich, he certainly acted like it. Maybe he could be convinced, since his interest in the unicorn fish was so keen.

Corrie saved her data in a secure folder and deleted it off the lab computer. She walked back to her lab bench, thinking wistfully of Sucker, the giant octopus they had encountered on their last cruise. What wouldn't she give for a sample from it?

Footsteps sounded in the hall of the lab. Corrie looked around, feeling jumpy even though she wasn't doing anything suspicious. Her thoughts of Sucker felt like they were written across her face.

Dr. Jonathan Chang, her master's degree supervisor, hailed her.

"Corrie, hello."

He was tanned, and the skin on his balding head looked sunburned. Corrie blinked. Was it Friday already? Jonathan was due back from a conference in a tropical locale.

"Hi, Jonathan. How was Hawaii?" She felt a pang of jealousy, which was quickly washed away by her satisfaction over her cruise on the *Clicker*. She would take a thousand unicorn fish over Hawaiian beaches, any day.

"Good, good. I spoke with Robert Norris from Scripps, and he had some ideas about your metabolites. I'll forward you his email and you can connect." He nodded at her lab bench. "How is the analysis going? Any results to show me yet?"

"Actually, yes." Corrie had been working hard during normal hours on her master's degree project. Unicorn fish were amazing, but the work she was supposed to be doing took precedence. She did have a genuine interest in it, after all, and next week on the *Clicker* she planned to spend much of her time sampling anemones for the bacteria they housed. "It's all very preliminary, of course, and I'll get more concrete data soon, but it looks like output of the metabolic product may vary on a salinity gradient."

"Excellent. I look forward to seeing your figures next week." He tapped his fingers on the lab bench briefly. "When you were on the boat, you sent me some figures. There was a phylogenetic tree attached to one of your emails, except it showed salmonids, not bacteria. What was that?"

Corrie's breath caught in her throat. How had she been so careless? She had sent Jonathan data from the unicorn fish. What must he think of it? It clearly showed the unknown sample as a different species. She tried to look puzzled.

"My mistake. That was a friend's tree, not mine. I must have attached it by accident."

Jonathan frowned at her.

"It was very intriguing. Did you notice? It looked like the test sample was an unidentified species nested in the salmonids."

Corrie chuckled to hide her unease.

"Yeah, he sent it to me for a laugh. It was major contamination, but it looked so real. Crazy, right?"

To her relief, Jonathan looked disappointed.

"Indeed. That's a good lesson for us, to make sure to double-check everything we do, and test all methods thoroughly. Things that are too good to be true usually are."

When Jonathan left the lab, Corrie sagged against the bench and rested her head on her arm. That was close. Too close. She couldn't afford to slip up like that, not unless she wanted to tell Jonathan everything.

And she didn't want to, not yet. She could hardly explain her reluctance, even to herself. Finding a new species was potentially the biggest discovery in decades, and she was at the forefront. She felt guilty that she wasn't sharing it. Surely, the scientific community had a right to know.

But then she thought of the mermaid she had seen as a child, and her many years of watching, and waiting, and hoping. She had worked hard on her blog, analyzing legends and dissecting myths, pouring years into her passion. She needed answers for herself, first. She needed to know what was really going on before she involved anyone else. Why were the unicorn fish and Sucker emerging now, and with such frequency? If they were that numerous, someone would have seen them before now. They were coming from somewhere, and recently. She needed to find that out before she told Jonathan. She didn't want the discovery of this secret world wrested from her and out of her control before she had found the answers she sought. This was her mission.

ZEBALLOS

Zeballos Artino tucked into his burger with gusto. His friend Jules Elliot had even cooked fries, deep-fried in hot oil, a daunting and hazardous feat on the boat. Jules had grinned and said that he liked to live dangerously, and that nothing was too big a risk for good food. Zeb wouldn't have done it, but he appreciated the flavor.

"It's quiet without Corrie and Krista," Jules said, poking a fry into ketchup.

"Yeah," Zeb said without elaboration. Sometimes the boat had felt too crowded with four people on board, especially when chatty grad student Corrie Duval had got going, or when his sister Krista Artino had scolded him. But now that he and Jules were alone on the *Clicker*, his father's old fishing vessel that he had inherited when the old man had died, Zeb found himself missing the women's busyness and chatter.

At least there were sea creatures to see. It had only been a few days, but Zeb had caught glimpses of the unicorn fish he called strolias on every dive so far. He even thought he'd seen a flash of tentacle from a brigar, the giant octopus as big as the *Clicker*. It had been dark, though, so he couldn't be sure.

"Where are we going now?" Jules asked through a mouthful of fries. Zeb chewed and pondered the question, then he put down his burger and tugged a map out of a crowded pouch on the wall beside the table. He spread it out and looked at it carefully.

"The west coast of Vancouver Island," he said finally. He pointed at a penciled star halfway up the large island. "There's an underwater reef that my mum mentioned in one of her stories. I'm pretty sure she meant the one here. I want to check it out."

"Okay," Jules said. He dipped a fry in ketchup. "Just as well we're heading that way. The strait is getting busy with summer coming. Tourists," he said with exaggerated disdain. "Hogging all the best anchor spots. Nobody bothers with the west coast."

"Because it's too rough, that's why," Zeb said absently, still tracing their path to the reef. What would he see there?

"Lucky I have an iron stomach, and I've never seen you vomit in my life," said Jules. He looked contemplatively at his fry, then shrugged and popped it in his mouth. "We'll be fine."

Zeb sprinkled salt on his fries and took a bite. The salt sizzled pleasantly on his tongue. He rubbed his arm to relieve the prickling sensation there. Jules looked at Zeb's hand and frowned.

"Do you need to swim again?" he asked. Zeb looked at his own hand in surprise. He hadn't consciously noticed the motion.

"I don't know. Maybe. Yes."

"Why so often lately?" Jules asked. "You never used to do this. Not that I knew about, anyway."

"No, I didn't." Swimming in the ocean was always a favorite hobby of Zeb's, from when he was old enough to hang onto his mother's neck while she swam, but it had never been a nagging need the way it sometimes felt these days. He didn't understand it, but it was easy enough to comply. They were on a boat, after all.

Zeb swallowed the rest of his burger and stood.

"I'm going to see what I can see. When I get back, we can pack up and head west."

"Roger that, captain," said Jules.

Zeb stopped at the galley on his way and reached into a high cupboard to extract two pieces of dried jellyfish. It was a favorite snack of his, and coincidentally, also of the strolias. Maybe, if they were feeling shy, he could entice them closer with their preferred treat. He liked making friends down there. On land, Jules was the outgoing one, but Zeb could communicate with the sea creatures much better than with his fellow humans. It was partly body positioning, partly certain noises, but he had a knack for it. It was nothing as amazing as his mother had been capable of, but the fish seemed to like him.

Zeb stuck a piece of jellyfish in his mouth and chewed the rubbery snack while he stripped to his swimsuit and shoved his feet into short red flippers. He carefully palmed the other jellyfish, put the ladder on the side of the boat so he could climb up later, then dived off the edge.

The water enveloped him in a cool embrace, as it always did. The itching, prickling sensation in his skin instantly faded, and his heartbeat slowed. Zeb smiled as wide as he could with his mouth closed. It just felt so good down here, so right.

Everything was green with an algae bloom caused by the warm spring sun, and he could hardly see further than his outstretched arm. It didn't matter, though, not to him. He did a quick somersault for fun, then closed his eyes and listened to the whisper of movement against his skin. Tiny differences in salinity, temperature, and motion painted him a picture of his surroundings more clearly than his eyes could ever do in these conditions.

He heard a pulse of sound, almost at the edge of his range, but he ignored it. He wasn't sure what it was, but it wasn't as relevant as the motion he felt below him. There was a school of fish, maybe as long as his forearm, rising steadily toward him. His heart leaped when he sensed a disturbance at the front of each fish's head, as though a horn sliced through the water.

Zeb opened his eyes in time to see seven strolias emerge from the murk. Their iridescent scales glimmered, even in the low light of the bloom. Zeb smiled again and held out the piece of jellyfish. Most hung back, but one bold strolia darted forward and snatched the piece from his fingers. It gulped it in one swallow.

Zeb rolled slowly over to see what the strolia would do. It hesitated, then repeated Zeb's action. He was elated and about to repeat the roll when he felt a movement on his skin. The strolias darted away and left Zeb alone to decipher what fish he felt approaching.

It was as long as he was, sleek and fast, but Zeb couldn't figure anything else out. It was headed straight to him, though, so he would find out soon enough. His stomach clenched in anticipation.

The creature slowed and approached him slowly. Out of the gloom, a head appeared. Zeb relaxed his shoulders in disappointment. It was a small shark, nothing more. He had expected something from his mother's legends, not a mundane shark.

But what kind of shark was it? It was too large for a dogfish, the small reef sharks that frequented these waters, and its prominent dorsal fin excluded it from being a six-gill shark. It was too small and not quite the right shape for a great white shark, and they tended to stay offshore. It wasn't a thresher shark with its oddly long tail.

Zeb caught a glimpse of distinct spots on the shark's top side, patches of coloration that didn't match any shark he knew about. His heartbeat quickened to almost the rate it pulsed on land. This was a *kroll*, the reef sharks from his mother's stories. Krolls had a poisonous bite but paired it with a placid temperament. They tended to be solitary or swim in small groups of two or three. This one was alone.

They were similar enough to other sharks, however, that Zeb understood how they could pass undetected. The same couldn't be said for strolias, nor the brigar. Where were these creatures coming from, and why now? He hoped the reef would give him some answers. For now, he had a chance to see a kroll, and that was excitement enough.

He rumbled deep in his chest, loud enough to vibrate the water for the kroll's sensitive pressure organs to pick up. The kroll circled back and looked at him out of one eye as it passed. Zeb rumbled again and held out a hand. The kroll passed by again and rubbed its sandpapery skin against Zeb's palm. Zeb winced but held firm with a wide grin. A few weeks ago, he would never have expected to touch a kroll. It was worth an abraded palm to do that.

CORRIE

Corrie heaved a hamper of clothes onto her bed and sat heavily beside it to fold the clothes. She'd finally done her laundry from her time on the boat. It had taken her over a week. She had been ridiculously busy the past week with cleaning gear and analyzing samples. Her supervisor wanted her to apply for a conference in the summer, but she needed data first. On top of that, she was running analyses on her unicorn fish samples when no one else was looking, which was often in the evening. Tonight was the first break she'd given herself.

The voices of her roommates floated through the thin walls, but Corrie ignored the temptation to talk and focused instead on her laundry. Housework was a pain, but it had to be done. There was no way she could leave an unfolded basket of clothes in her room. It would eat away at her tidy mind until she had put away everything. She could socialize soon.

She picked up a tee shirt and folded it. She'd worn this one during their battle with Sucker, the giant octopus that they'd called upon to distract Matt Nielsen in his makeshift drug lab. Sucker had been a mixed blessing, since it had nearly taken them out along with the lab, but they had escaped in the end.

Corrie remembered Zeb's disappearance during the skirmish, and his reappearance soaking wet without shoes. He had said he would distract Sucker. What had he done? Surely, he hadn't jumped in the water. But if he had been pushed by a tentacle and submersed by accident, how had he removed his shoes? And he hadn't been cold at all on the ride back to the *Clicker*, even though the water was frigid and the wind brisk. She would have been shivering hard enough for her teeth to clack together.

Corrie laid the tee shirt aside and plucked socks out of the hamper. She carefully laid one on top of the other and folded the pair together. The Sucker incident hadn't been the only unexplained absence of Zeb's. Numerous times she'd tried to find him on the boat, only to be waylaid by his friend Jules and his sister Krista. He might have been in the engine room, as they had claimed, but she got the sense that they were hiding something. The three of them clearly went way back, and there were things she was not privy to.

That was fair enough, Corrie mused, since she'd only known them for a week. But it still felt suspicious. What would they need to hide? And, for that matter, what was with Zeb's backstory? He had tried to pass himself off as a rich kid blowing his inheritance on a hobby project, but there were so many holes in that story. The fish boat was an unlikely acquisition, and Zeb's rough clothing was hardly the apparel of a millionaire. But if he wasn't rich, how could he afford to be on the boat and not work? And why would he pretend to be rich and offer the award?

Corrie picked up the slinky shirt she had worn to the island pub and smoothed it out. That brought her back to an important point: Zeb's intense investment in the unicorn fish. It was far greater than Jules, who viewed the fish as an oddity, or Krista, who actively discouraged an interest. Zeb's fascination was on par with her own and possibly exceeded it, if that were possible. He took great pains to hide his excitement, though. Why?

And why was Krista so worried about him?

Corrie stood and placed her folded clothes in her chest of drawers. There were more mysteries aboard the *Clicker* than just the unicorn fish, that was certain. Maybe she would find out more next week, when she boarded the boat once more. Zeb was keen to go out again, and she wasn't going to pass up another amazing opportunity to collect samples. Her supervisor had been baffled, but agreeable.

She was almost ready to join her roommates for some much-needed gab time, but she flipped open her laptop quickly to check the comments from her recent blog post. She'd written an abbreviated version of her adventures on the *Clicker*, careful to avoid names and places, and she was keen to read its reception.

There were plenty of "amazing" and "cool" comments, which she scrolled through quickly with a smile. A slightly longer comment made her pause, from someone labeled "MC."

What a unique find. Where did you see the unicorn fish? I'd give anything to dive down and see one in person.

Corrie frowned. There was no way she would tell anyone details of the fish. Her main purpose in making it public on her site was to see if anyone else had heard of a unicorn fish before. She didn't want others to catch their own or go down the path of Matt Nielsen. She wanted to keep the unicorn fish safe and private for now. She felt confident that no one with any real clout followed her blog—it was a fantastical subject, after all—but MC's comment made her pause.

She wasn't sure how to respond, so she closed her laptop and headed to the kitchen. It was time to reconnect with her real-life friends.

ADRIANNA

Sophie Trip crunched a chip in the kitchen of their shared house and shook her head in amazement.

"I can't believe you and Patrick have been dating for a year already. What are you still doing in this house with us? I mean, I know we're amazing roommates, but if I had to choose between us and my man, well." Trip laughed. "An on-call man would win, hands-down."

"You're terrible," Adrianna Rhodes replied. "I know, it's time. We're looking for a place, actually. His suite is too small for me, and this house is maxed out with us four. The right apartment will come up soon, I have a good feeling."

Trip pouted.

"I'll miss you."

Adrianna held up her hand, and they tapped their chips together.

"Me too. But I'm not gone yet. Don't rush me."

Corrie moseyed into the kitchen, looking hungry for chips and conversation. Trip held out the bag and Corrie dived her hand in gratefully.

"Where have you been, stranger?" Trip said. "We haven't seen you much since your pleasure cruise."

"Ha, it was not that at all," Corrie said through a mouthful. She swallowed. "I worked damn hard and forgot to sleep. And I collected so many samples that I've been at the lab every evening since. Don't let anyone tell you that science is for slackers."

"Hear, hear," said Trip.

"Tell us about your little cruise," Adrianna said. Corrie snorted, but Adrianna just smiled, her attempt to make Corrie laugh successful. "Swimming in crystal waters, drinking with pool boys, the usual?"

"Scuba diving in freezing green waters and watching water

filter, you mean?" Corrie grinned. "No, it was great. I dived two or three times a day and collected so many anemone samples I hardly know what to do with them all. Some of my results look really interesting so far, but I won't get a full picture until all the data come back."

Adrianna waited. When Corrie reached for more chips, clearly finished speaking, Adrianna spoke.

"That's it? A whole week away, and that's all you have to say? It's very unlike you."

Corrie shrugged defensively.

"What do you want to know?"

Trip laughed.

"Normally, you wouldn't be able to stop talking about something like this. Did a fish get your tongue?"

Corrie looked uncomfortable for a moment, then her face smoothed. Adrianna rescued her.

"Tell us some gossip. What was the crew like?"

"There were four of us," Corrie replied, seemingly happy to have a topic to latch on to. "Krista is Zeb's sister, the captain's sister. She took some breaking in—maybe I was horning in on her territory, I don't know—but I won her over."

"That's my girl," Trip said with approval.

"Jules is Zeb's friend. He was great. Good for a chat—Zeb's quiet, and Krista took a while to warm up—and oh man, can he cook. It was amazing."

"Got to love a man who knows his way around the kitchen," said Trip with an appreciative smack of her lips.

"Jules was great, was he?" Adrianna said, a teasing note in her voice. "Yummy great?"

"Good-looking, in a disheveled way," Corrie said with a laugh.

"What about this Zeb character?" Adrianna said. Corrie paused, and Adrianna wondered what was going through her mind.

"He's quiet—"

"You said that already," Trip said. Adrianna waved her away.

"Go on, Corrie."

"He's fine, nice. I don't know."

"You're being shifty," said Trip. "What are you not telling us?"

Corrie looked uncomfortable. Adrianna leaned forward.

"Do you like him?"

"Why are you trying to set me up with everyone?" Corrie asked with a laugh. "Aren't I already dating David?"

Adrianna leaned back against the counter with a grin and a wave of defeat, but she noticed Corrie's eyes didn't match her smile. Her deflection of Adrianna's question had been deft. She wondered what had really happened on the boat, and what Corrie truly thought of the mysterious captain.

"At least tell us if he was hot," said Trip, not willing to let the topic slide. Corrie squirmed.

"I guess so."

Adrianna jumped to save Corrie.

"So, you dived and sampled and did lab work? That's it?"

"That's a science cruise for you," said Corrie with a look of relief at the shift in topic. "We did go to a pub on a remote island once, so thanks for making me pack that skirt."

"Ha, I knew it," Adrianna said in triumph. "Always be prepared—"

"To look good," Trip finished with her. They all laughed.

JULES

They were finally heading up the west coast of Vancouver Island, and Jules was reorganizing the galley. They might encounter rougher seas out here, without any land to block the ocean swells that were created in Pacific storms far offshore. It paid to have a few dinner plans that didn't need much preparation, in case cooking was too difficult. He wasn't fond of those meals, but necessity was the mother of invention, and he had some decent menus in mind for rough days. He wanted to try a new recipe for Cuban grilled salmon with avocado salsa, modified to be cooked in a single pan that he could hold steady during rolling waves. He relished the challenge.

Jules knelt on the floor to extract a can of beans from the back of the low cupboard that was too deep to be truly useful but was large enough that he couldn't ignore the needed space in his crowded galley. Something clicked under his fingers as he scrambled for the rolling can. His fingers closed around the wayward cylinder.

"Ah ha," he said in triumph. "Gotcha."

The boat engine throttled down, and the anchor chain clanked. Jules arranged errant cans to his satisfaction. After the engine stopped completely, Zeb popped his head into the galley.

"What are you doing, alphabetizing your cans?" Zeb said. "Surely you can't organize any more. It's all you do."

"It's a complicated place, this galley," said Jules in defense from his undignified position on the floor. "It's a well-oiled machine and must be tended with care for best performance."

Zeb rolled his eyes.

"I'll take your word for it. I'm going for a swim, see what creatures are here. After yesterday's sightings, I can't wait to see what this stretch has in store."

"Good luck," Jules said. "Wait. Catch me a lingcod for

dinner, will you? It's been ages since we had fresh fish."

"If by ages, you mean three days, then sure. I'll get the harpoon gun."

Jules waved off his comment, and Zeb disappeared. With the promise of lingcod, Jules prepped vegetables and rice. Then, with nothing he truly needed to do, he grabbed his phone and headphones and set up a chair on the aft deck. With his feet on the bulwark and music pounding in his ears, Jules was content.

A half hour later, Zeb climbed onto the deck with a lingcod hanging by its gills from his fingers. Jules grinned at the prospect of dinner, then he saw Zeb's despondent face and his grin slipped. He removed his headphones.

"What happened to you? It looks like someone died."

"I didn't see anything," Zeb said in a hollow voice. "Not a damn thing. How could the ocean be teeming with strolias and krolls one day, and empty the next? It doesn't make sense."

"There's a lot about all this that doesn't make sense," Jules said, trying to inject a reasonable note into this conversation. "We're talking about legendary creatures. If they are so abundant, why does hardly anyone catch them? Besides, we were in a different spot yesterday. Maybe they don't like it here."

"Maybe." Zeb didn't look convinced, but he allowed Jules to take the fish from his fingers and heave it in his arms. Jules didn't like to see him so down, not after his excitement from all the sightings. Zeb had spent too long being glum and withdrawn after his father's death. Jules wracked his brains for something comforting to say but could only come up with his specialty.

"Let me cook this bad boy. You'll feel better after dinner."

FLINT

Flint straightened his tie. The damn thing was askew again. He didn't know how his colleague Gavin always kept his so immaculate, no matter what their job was. He probably glued it into place. Flint snickered under his breath. That would be just like Gavin.

"Care to share what amuses you?" Gavin said from the driver's seat of their company SUV. Flint shook his head.

"You wouldn't find it funny." He checked the map on his phone. "Finally, we're almost there. Why does this loser live out here? I swear, we passed the middle of nowhere hours ago."

"That was quite witty," said Gavin. "Was that a spur-of-the-moment comment, or did you prepare it in advance?"

"Whatever." Flint glowered for a moment. Gavin was such a jerk sometimes. He did his job well, though, and they were a good team. Flint trusted him. He just didn't like him all the time. "What are we trying to get out of this guy, again?"

Gavin let out a long-suffering sigh.

"I briefed you on the ferry, if you recall, but I can repeat the instructions. The man we are visiting, Mathias Nielsen, knows where to find the enhancer that Mr. Callahan desires. We enter his home, and I ask him politely to tell us what we want to know." Gavin sniffed. "If he is not cooperative, you are authorized to help him understand our intentions."

"All right." Flint cracked his knuckles. "I'm up."

"When I give the signal, not before. And must you make that terrible noise? It's quite disgusting."

"I'm preparing. I'm here to give my job my best performance. Are you going to stop me?"

Gavin subsided into a dissatisfied silence. Flint grinned and checked the map again.

"Turn left here," he said. "Looks like it's that little white house."

Gavin pulled over and stopped the engine. They stared at the house for a minute. Although it was dinnertime, the early summer sun was still high in the sky. There was a red pickup truck in the driveway, and a window box held a row of petunias. Gavin turned to Flint.

"Are you ready?"

"Ready and willing." Flint cracked his knuckles again for the joy of seeing Gavin's repulsed expression. "Let's do it."

Gavin led the way to the front door. Raised voices floated through an open window.

"It wasn't that much! Honestly, Matt," said a petulant woman's voice.

"How much do you think I earn?" a man's deep voice growled.

"Apparently, not enough." The woman's voice was snide. "My job at the restaurant pays more. Maybe you should apply to be a busboy there."

"Then buy your own damn ring," the man shouted. The fluttering of paper being waved through air drifted through the open window. "If you want a rock as big as your head, you picked the wrong guy."

"Maybe I did," the woman said quietly but with menace.

Flint and Gavin looked at each other. Gavin raised his eyebrow with amusement.

"We'll likely need your expertise sooner rather than later," he said. "An angry man is difficult to reason with."

"Excellent." Flint cracked his knuckles again. Gavin shook his head and knocked firmly on the door.

A moment later, the door swung open. A woman with teased blond hair and full breasts, amplified by a tight-fitting top, glared at them.

"Can I help you?" she said without any of the happy politeness that phrase is usually accompanied by. Gavin nodded.

"Indeed. We need to speak to Mathias Nielsen on urgent business." He stepped forward in a deferential but determined manner that always defeated those in his way. The woman stepped back with confusion on her face.

"Matt? There are two men here to see you." She shook her head and suspicion entered her eyes. "What were your names?"

"Our names aren't important," Gavin said politely. He breezed by her, and Flint followed him into the house. They were in a small living room populated with an overstuffed loveseat, chair, and a television mounted on the wall. A big man stood at the far end, huge and blond and menacing-looking. Flint couldn't help his smile. The man would be a challenge.

Flint loved a challenge.

He patted his sides to check that the tools of his trade were in their correct positions, then he waited for Gavin's signal. By the glower in the big man's eyes, it wouldn't be long.

"Mathias Nielsen," Gavin began. "Our employer wishes to know more about the product called Sea Salt. He would be obliged if you divulged everything you know."

"Piss off," Matt said. "I don't have to tell you anything. Who are you, anyway, barging into my house? Get out of here."

"Sea Salt?" the woman said to Matt. "What are they talking about?"

"It doesn't matter, Bianca," he replied without looking at her. "It's all over now, anyway."

"That's not strictly true," Gavin said pleasantly. "Our employer is still interested. We would like the information, please."

"Maybe you didn't hear me the first time." Matt stepped forward until he stood in front of Gavin. He looked down at the smaller man to intimidate him. "Piss. Off."

He was too close for comfort to Gavin, but the perfect distance for Flint. Gavin's eyes flicked to Flint, and he nodded.

Flint smiled, then struck.

Matt hadn't been looking at Flint, and that was his downfall. The punch to his gut doubled him over with a cough, and Flint didn't let him recover. Recovery of an informant gave him power, and giving an informant power wasn't in Mr. Callahan's best interests. Flint was, if nothing else, a loyal employee.

With a series of kicks and punches in strategic places, Flint soon had the larger man sprawled, wheezing, on the loveseat. The woman, Bianca, screamed in soundtrack and edged to the door.

"Stay put, please," Gavin said smoothly. "Bianca, was it? My associate prefers not to threaten women, but he will do what is necessary during our negotiations."

"I'm not that picky, really," said Flint from his position beside Matt, his switchblade pressing into the big man's throat.

Bianca whimpered and halted her progress to the exit.

Flint was a little disappointed—he thought he might need some of his other tools—but Matt had gone down easier than expected. Flint's handy switchblade had done the trick. He supposed there was no need to complicate things when simple tools got the job done.

"Are you ready to tell us what we want to know?" said Gavin in the same pleasant tone he had used before Flint's attack. Matt glared at him with murder in his eyes and spat a curse at him.

Gavin sighed with disappointment and nodded at Flint. Flint smiled and pressed the switchblade into Matt's neck.

Bianca shrieked again. Matt shrank into the loveseat and a small line of red blood dribbled down his neck.

"Okay, okay!" Matt said with a gasp. "It doesn't matter that much. I'll tell you."

"Excellent," Gavin said with a satisfied smile. "Excellent decision, Mr. Nielsen. Please, don't hold back."

"There's a weird fish with a horn on its head," Matt said, his eyes resigned. "Looks like a mutant salmon. It's covered in slime. When you eat the slime, it gives you hallucinations above water, but extra strength and speed underwater." Matt frowned. "How did you know about the enhancer, anyway?"

"We hear many things," Gavin said. Matt's eyes closed briefly with understanding.

"I told Tom Banks. He can't keep a secret to save his life."

"What the hell is all this?" Bianca demanded in a shrill voice.

"Please stay out of this if you care for your boyfriend," Gavin said without deviating from his pleasant tone. Bianca's eyes widened, but she shrank against the wall and spoke no more. Gavin continued speaking to Matt. "And how do you catch these fish?"

Matt was silent for a long moment. Flint grew tired of waiting and backhanded the big man, who grunted with pain and glared at him. Flint jerked his head at Gavin.

"Answer him."

"Use dried jellyfish as bait. You can get it at Chinese specialty stores."

"You've been very helpful," said Gavin with a pleased nod. "Thank you. Who else knows about these fish?"

"You want me to rat out other people so you can beat them up, too?" Matt looked incredulous. Flint raised his hand and Matt flinched.

"Nobody needs to get hurt," said Gavin. "We're only after information. I assume your girlfriend here knows nothing, given her horrified and disbelieving expression. Who else?"

"I got the fish from Larry Eastman, but he doesn't know anything more than I do. Leave him out of this." Matt panted for a moment, then he looked hopeful. "Zeb Artino, Krista's brother. He owns the *Clicker* now. It's a fishboat. He and his crew were following me around, harassing me about the fish. I think they know something, but I don't know what. They smashed up my lab," he added with indignation.

Gavin nodded at Flint, who removed the switchblade from Matt's neck with a twinge of regret. He had so many skills and rarely got to use them. Maybe one day he would find a worthy opponent. It was unfortunate—the big man had shown such promise.

Gavin walked with unhurried steps to the fridge, visible from the living room where they stood. He pulled out a whiteboard marker from his pocket and wrote "Tangled Net" and his cell phone number on the front of the fridge.

"Call me if you remember anything else," Gavin said to Matt. He beckoned to Flint. "Come, we're done here."

Flint followed Gavin out of the door. When it had slammed shut behind him, Bianca's voice started.

"Matty! Are you okay?"

There was an indistinct muttering followed by a slap.

"That's for keeping secrets from me," Bianca shouted. "What the hell were you thinking?"

Flint shook his head with a grin. He wouldn't be in Matt's oversized shoes right now for all the money in the world. A wronged woman was a terrifying creature indeed.

ZEBALLOS

Zeb closed the cabin door behind him with a sigh. He didn't know why he was so despondent after seeing no unusual fish. After all, he'd lived almost his whole life without spotting a single creature from his mother's stories, and now they popped up almost every time he went underwater. It was only to be expected that they wouldn't show occasionally.

Something was different, though. He couldn't pin the sensation down, but in the ocean this afternoon there was a shift in the currents or tone of ocean sounds that spoke of change. Did it mean that the creatures were gone for good?

He shook his head to clear it of negative thoughts and reached for a cardboard moving box among several that he'd stashed on the top bunk. Since Krista and Corrie were no longer on the *Clicker*, Jules had taken over their cabin. As he had succinctly put it, "Sharing a cabin is fun in a summer-camp sort of way, but a man needs some privacy." Zeb agreed, although he missed Jules' steady breathing in the quiet of the night. Now, his thoughts plagued him without any distraction.

The boxes were from his apartment in Campbell River, four of the many that movers had deposited in his small one-bedroom from his father's house after he had died. Krista had packed the house up while he had dealt with the boat transfer papers, and she had said she didn't want any of it. It was up to Zeb to keep or trash the rest. He would have told her to toss it all in the nearest dumpster if he hadn't wondered if anything of his mother's was hiding in the flotsam of his father's life.

So, several towering stacks of boxes filled his little space. He'd been ignoring them, not wanting to go through and dredge up memories. He didn't want to remember bad memories, but, even worse, he didn't want to feel nostalgia for his father. He wanted to hold onto his anger and frustration over the secrets George Artino had kept. It was easier than forgiveness.

He wanted the boxes gone, though. His apartment was small enough without piles of cardboard looming over his couch. Last week, when he and Jules had docked the boat to do laundry and sleep a night at their respective homes, the boxes had been overwhelming. In the morning, he had grabbed a stack and fled their overbearing presence.

Zeb placed the box on the lower bunk and sat next to it. He didn't know how to prepare himself. Would the contents be too much to handle? He almost stood and left the cabin but then mentally shook himself. Searching through each box wouldn't happen by itself. He steeled his nerves and cracked open the cardboard flaps.

It was anticlimactic. The box was filled with literal junk: receipts, old grocery store value cards, empty keychains, a shoehorn. He recognized the contents of his father's kitchen drawer, the one where detritus went to die. Zeb blew air through pursed lips and sifted the junk between his fingers. There wasn't anything of his mother in here, and beyond a reminder of George's messy housekeeping, not much of his father either. If all the boxes were this easy, the task shouldn't take long. It was almost too bad he hadn't started earlier. He could have cleared out his space of the reminder of George Artino's death sooner.

Zeb's fingers touched metal, and he pulled the item out. It was another keychain, this one of a smiling metal whale that said, "I love BC." Zeb snorted. He couldn't picture his father ever using such a keychain. He must have received it for free.

There was a key on this ring, though. What was it for? Zeb looked closer, mystified. In tiny letters on the head, the words "Dan's Storage" were engraved.

What had his father been doing with a storage locker? Zeb groaned at the thought of more junk squirreled away, then he frowned. George's house, while modest, would have had plenty of room to fit more items. Why would his father, a consummate miser, have spent money on renting a locker? It didn't make sense.

Zeb's curiosity was piqued, and he slipped the key into his wallet. He would have to look up Dan's Storage. The next time he was nearby, he wanted to see what his father considered valuable enough to store away from the house.

Zeb sat in the chair in the wheelhouse, occasionally touching the wheel to keep course, but otherwise letting the boat go on its own. Jules lounged in the foldout chair next to him, flipping through a months-old fishing magazine.

"Why did your dad have these? They're so boring." Jules flipped through a few pages at once. "Seriously, how many ways can you talk about the big one that got away? Or review the best new fishing equipment? It doesn't seem like your old man's thing."

"It wasn't," Zeb replied, leaning back in his chair. "He went to the corner store and bought whatever he thought the charter people might like. There are a few diving magazines around, too. At least the underwater photography is good in those ones."

"Maybe if all the pictures were like this one." Jules held up a page with an advertisement for fishing line, shown off by a young woman in a bikini holding a caught salmon. "Then I could understand it."

"You can stock the wheelhouse with your choice of reading material when we stop in a port next." Zeb rummaged beside him with a lazy hand, trying to reach his bag of dried jellyfish without moving from his comfortable perch. Jules stared at the photo.

"Man, I need a girlfriend." He closed the magazine and tossed it onto the counter behind Zeb. "I need a lot of things, but wishing never delivers, does it? It seems to be my fate to stay trapped on this boat with you for eternity, watching you eat those squidgy snacks." Zeb had finally found his jellyfish, and he opened his mouth to show Jules a piece clenched between his teeth. Jules shuddered. "Disgusting. I'm all for adventurous eating, believe me, but even I have limits."

"You don't know what you're missing." Zeb made a show of tossing a piece in the air and catching it with his open mouth. Jules looked away with an exaggerated shudder.

"That guy is a long way from port in that zippy little motorboat." Jules pointed at a flashy speedboat crossing their bow at a distance. "It looks more suited to waterskiing than sport fishing."

Zeb gave a disinterested shrug.

"You can sport fish from any boat, I guess." Zeb sat upright and looked closer at the boat. "Does the passenger have binoculars? Why is she looking at us?"

The woman in the back of the speedboat had binoculars trained on the *Clicker*. After a moment of scoping out their vessel, she turned to speak to the man driving the boat. He nodded, then they made a quick turn and sped away in the direction they had come from. Zeb looked at Jules in puzzlement.

"Friends of yours?"

"If I had friends with that boat, I wouldn't be skulking around on this old clunker." Jules frowned. "What did they want?"

"Searching for someone, I guess. When we weren't it, they went to find another boat." Zeb said the words, but he didn't quite believe them. It was stupid, but he couldn't shake the sense of unease that had settled in his stomach.

CORRIE

David struck the white cue ball with his billiard cue. It clacked against a striped ball which then ricocheted off the table edge and sunk into a hole. David clenched his fist in the air with satisfaction.

Corrie's mind drifted to her plans for tomorrow. She had a full day of lab work, starting at eight in the morning, and in her minimal downtime she wanted to look through her data so far, put it into graphical form and visualize it. She'd left her samples in a good state today, but there was so much more she needed to do, and she wanted to get on it.

"Your turn, Corrie," David said.

"Yes, of course." Corrie snapped out of her reverie and hoisted her cue onto the table. She eyed the configuration of balls, deciding what the best angle was for her to sink a solid color ball.

"Try standing here," David said, pointing beside him. "And aim for the six ball, see? You can hit it off the edge, here, and sink it into this hole." He pointed at the corner of the table.

Corrie bit her tongue. David was only trying to help, but she liked finding her own way, figuring out the game for herself. She wasn't great at it, but wasn't that the way to get better? David was excellent at billiards, though. He was only trying to help. She gave him a smile.

"Okay, I'll try it. Six ball, you're going down."

She moved next to David and lined up her shot. The cue ball flew toward the six ball, which bounced off the side and traveled to the corner. It rebounded next to the hole and came to a stop in the center of the table.

"That was really close," David said. "Maybe a little lighter next time. It was good, though. This is fun, a great way to spend our Wednesday date night."

David lined up his next shot. The cue ball cracked against a striped ball with a tight, smooth motion. After it sunk into a hole, he turned to Corrie.

"Guess what? I finally saved enough for a down payment," he said. Corrie beamed at him.

"Congratulations. I know you've been working at that."

"Thanks. I'm going condo shopping next week. Want to come along? It's good to have a second opinion, especially if you're going to be spending time there, too." He looked at her hopefully.

Corrie's brain ground to a halt. Did David mean what she thought he meant? In her opinion, they were way too new an item to be talking about moving in together. Adrianna and Patrick were only now talking about it, and they'd been dating for a year. Surely, that's not what he had meant. He had been speaking of her spending the night, not living with him. Her mind started working again, and she tried to keep her emotions off her face. Maybe she could take his words at face value.

That brought up another conundrum. Corrie couldn't think of anything more yawn-inducing than looking at condos for sale. Some people got great joy out of imagining themselves in a new home, she knew, but she was not one of them. She'd spent too many open houses doing homework in a corner while her realtor mother worked. She'd probably be renting forever, just so she wouldn't have to go through that hunt.

But it was important to David, so she gave him her best smile.

"Sounds great. I'm truly excited for you. Lab work has been crazy, but if I can manage the time, I will be there."

Privately, she wondered if she could schedule her sample processing so it coincided with condo-hunting. David looked happy, though, so Corrie decided to play it by ear. She could probably muster up enthusiasm for one or two places. A cheery thought occurred to her.

"Wait," she said. "I'll be heading out on the boat again next week, did I tell you? Hopefully we can squeeze a few viewings in before then."

David's face fell, although he tried to hide it.

"Wow, again? I thought you got lots of samples already."

"I got a good amount, but if I'm being offered another week of sampling for free? That's something I can't pass up."

What was his reaction about? This was an amazing opportunity on the heels of her previous one. She was a fortunate grad student, indeed. Why wasn't he seeing it?

"You made a good impression with the captain, I see," David said. He said it in a joking way, but it was too easy to hear the jealous undertones. Corrie finally understood what was going on, and her temper flared.

"Yes. I'm an excellent scientist, if I do say so myself," she said tersely. "It's nice when someone appreciates you for your hard work and dedication to your career. I enjoy the support."

David looked chastened, and Corrie relented. They were still new enough that maybe he didn't feel comfortable with her yet. She'd been away for a week, and busy after that, so they hadn't seen much of each other lately. Maybe it was only natural he felt unsure of her affections.

"Which ball should I try for now?" she asked to smooth over her abruptness. David brightened at the request for coaching.

"Your four ball is wide open. Looks like a clear shot. Hit it right from here."

They played another game, until Corrie got bored. She ran her hand along David's arm in a clear signal. It had been a while since they'd been intimate, and she was ready. Maybe he would feel more secure afterward, as well. He got the hint and quickly paid up, and they left in the direction of David's apartment.

Adrianna opened the fridge in their shared kitchen the next

day.

"I think there's some pasta sauce in here somewhere." She rummaged in the back. "I only opened it the other day."

"It'll do," said Corrie. "I'm too hungry to be picky. Is the water almost boiling? I found the spaghetti."

"Here it is," Adrianna said in triumph, brandishing the half-jar of tomato sauce. "I knew it." She placed it on the counter. Corrie pulled out a saucepan for her.

"It's nice we could have dinner tonight," Corrie said. "It's quiet with Koni vacationing in Japan and Trip out."

"Did she tell you? It's a hot date," Adrianna said. "Some guy she met at the bar. She wasn't super jazzed about him, but nothing ventured, nothing gained, right?"

"I guess," Corrie said. She wasn't convinced a dinner out was worth any price, but to each their own.

"Still working hard at the lab?" Adrianna asked, her focus on slicing carrots. Corrie leaned against the counter. It was nice to give her hands a break.

"You bet. I hope I survive this field season. Wait, I didn't tell you. I'm going out on the boat again next week. Zeb offered me another week of sampling."

"What?" Adrianna turned to look at Corrie. Her eyes were wide. "That's amazing! I'm so excited for you. How did you manage that?"

"I'm lucky, I guess," said Corrie. "It's so great. I'll have enough data for a whole chapter of my thesis, at least."

Adrianna went back to chopping her carrots, but she looked at Corrie with a sly, sideways glance.

"This Zeb seems like a really helpful guy."

"Yeah, he is." Corrie ignored Adrianna's subtext.

"He must be impressed by you," Adrianna said with greater emphasis. Corrie frowned.

"Honestly, Adrianna. It's nothing like that." She sighed. "Although, try convincing David of that. He seriously needs to loosen up. All I ask is a little trust. Do I really come across as someone who plays around?"

"Hardly." Adrianna's hands paused at her task. "But, are you really into David, or is he just a warm body? A placeholder boyfriend?"

Corrie sighed. She wasn't sure how to answer her roommate, because she wasn't sure of the answer herself. How did she feel about David? They got along well. He was good-looking, easy to talk to, and happy to please her. What was she looking for, if not that?

"I don't know. He's what I need." She thought of Dylan, an ex-boyfriend who was everything she didn't need, and her resolve for appreciating David's attributes strengthened. "He's good for me."

"But is he what you want?" Adrianna said gently.

"I don't know. Maybe. Sometimes what I want isn't what I should want." Corrie changed the topic, which was steering too close to uncomfortable truths for her. "What have you been up to lately?"

Adrianna seemed content to change the subject, for which Corrie was grateful. She didn't have time or energy for soul-searching right now. Maybe when her sampling and analysis calmed down, she could think about her life a bit more. For now, David was right for her. And maybe for longer, who knew. She pushed spaghetti into the pot of now-boiling water and swirled it around.

"Did I tell you?" Adrianna said. "I went to Patrick's work party on the weekend. You remember, he's been freelancing for that tech magazine, and they gave him a remote position last month? But it was so much more than a work party. You should have seen this place, Cor." Adrianna shook her head slowly in amazement. "Patrick's boss owns a private island in the strait. A private island, can you imagine? There was a boat shuttle to get us to the island, and it ran back and forth all evening to take people home after. And the house! Amazing. Views off a cliff, ocean forever, gorgeous forest behind, a rocky beach on one side, just glorious."

"Must be nice to have tons of coin," Corrie said with a smile. If she had that much money, she probably wouldn't spend it on a private island—too isolated for her—but the beach sounded nice.

"Insane. There was a whole building dedicated to an indoor pool. I mean, wow. And, get this: a private aquarium."

"No big deal," Corrie said with a giggle. "I have a private aquarium, too."

"I'm talking much bigger than your ten-gallon fish tank. No, a serious aquarium. As in, shark-sized. Multiple sharks. This guy is a private collector of sea animals. There's a whole room lined with ceiling-high tanks. It's incredible. You'd love it."

"I'd love to see it, that's for sure." Corrie wondered how big the tanks were to contain a fish like a shark, which had to swim constantly to breathe. She hoped the tanks were as big as Adrianna claimed.

"And he had some fish that I didn't recognize," Adrianna said. Corrie's focus sharpened. What did Adrianna mean? "Not that I know my sea life as well as you do, but I've taken my share of biology courses, and I didn't recognize some of them. Crazy fish. I don't know where he got them all."

"That sounds incredible," Corrie said, trying to keep her excitement at a normal-sounding level. The fish Adrianna had seen were probably unusual, not mythical. Nevertheless, Corrie longed to see them with her own eyes. "I'd love to see it."

"That reminds me. You came up in conversation."

"Me?"

"Yes, when we were talking to Miles—that's Patrick's boss' name, Miles Callahan—you came up in conversation."

"How did that happen?" Corrie said with a laugh. "I'm not that interesting."

"Sure, you are," Adrianna said. "I think what you do is fascinating. I think all my friends are amazing. Miles was interested, probably because he collects fish and you're a marine biologist. Anyway, Miles was great to talk to. We all really hit it off. He even said he'd invite us back sometime for a private tour of his aquarium when there were fewer people around." Adrianna tasted the pasta sauce. "Warm enough. I'm sure he was only being polite, so I won't hold my breath for an invitation."

"Here's hoping." Corrie pulled two plates out of the cupboard. "It sounds like a beautiful place to revisit."

"Totally. Patrick loves Miles, can't say enough good things about him. He runs the magazine, but I think he gets his real money from investment schemes. He finds opportunities and grows them, somehow."

Corrie spooned pasta sauce on top of two plates of spaghetti.

"I hope you get to go back. I'll have to be satisfied with my little tank and my pleco, Hot Lips. He may not be exotic, but he's mine."

They took their plates to the table, but Corrie wondered about the fish in Miles Callahan's aquarium. Was she overly sensitive about strange-looking fish after her adventures on the *Clicker*, or did Miles have something she would want to see?

JULES

They'd finally made it to the reef north of Tofino that Zeb was certain his mother had mentioned in a story. Jules didn't know if Zeb truly remembered much from back then—he could hardly remember his classmates from elementary school, let alone the minutiae from bedtime stories—but Zeb was convinced, and that was good enough for Jules. He was just there to cook and make sure Zeb didn't do anything stupid in his despondency. His obsession was all-consuming, and someone had to think of the details. Zeb would probably eat nothing but those horrible jellyfish snacks for breakfast, lunch, and dinner, and that was a crime against cooking. There was hardly any nutrition in them, either—Jules had checked the packaging of the disgusting things. Jules had been tempted to add them to something, maybe sliced in a risotto, but he couldn't bring himself to ruin a tasty side dish with them. Zeb would simply have to eat them on his own.

Zeb dived in to check out the reef, and Jules settled onto the bow with a rolled towel under his head. He closed his eyes and enjoyed the sun. They were having paninis for lunch, but he'd already prepped grilled vegetables and sliced cheese so he could assemble and cook the sandwiches when Zeb returned.

It was quiet here, on this lonely stretch of coast. The sea was rough and tossed the *Clicker* unpleasantly, but Zeb didn't want to take shelter in a cove until he'd checked out the reef. Jules had a strong stomach, so he spread his limbs on the deck and let the boat rock him under the sun.

The sound of a motor stirred him twenty minutes later. He sat up, wondering who would bother coming out here. An expensive-looking white liveaboard puttered nearby. Fishing lines draped past the stern, indicating it was likely a private fishing charter. Jules lay down again. He hoped Zeb had sense enough to not touch the fishhook. He snickered at the thought of them baiting with dried jellyfish. Zeb would have a hard time passing up that.

By the time Zeb padded onto the deck, dripping and downhearted with his failure to see any strange fish, Jules had lunch ready. They ate on the aft deck. Zeb stared at his plate for a moment—Jules had placed a few pieces of jellyfish on the side to cheer him up—then he took a piece of the snack with a glance of recognition at Jules.

The fishing charter motored by again. Black lettering on the pristine white hull named the boat the *Discoverer*.

"I wonder if they're having any luck," Jules said.

"Lots of greenlings down there," Zeb said. "If they have the right bait."

"They've already been by here before. Do they think they'll have better luck the second time?"

Zeb chewed and stared at the boat with a frown. His concern made Jules look twice at the motorboat, but it didn't hold any significance to him.

"Weird," Zeb said finally. "Let's move along a few kilometers north. The reef extends that way."

"Aye aye, captain."

They moved further north after lunch. While Jules held their position, Zeb went for a quick dive. Once again, the charter boat trolled past them, too far away for Jules to make out features of the people fishing. He felt uneasy but couldn't place why. Zeb's mood must be affecting him.

"The charter was back," he said casually when Zeb entered the wheelhouse after his dive. "Again."

"Do you think—" Zeb paused. "That maybe we're being followed?"

"Maybe if I had an ego the size of yours, I'd think it," said Jules with an attempt at joviality. "Why would anyone follow us?"

"I don't know," said Zeb with a pensive look at the rolling waves. "Ever since that motorboat turned around at the sight of us, I've felt on edge."

Jules couldn't say anything against this, for he felt the same way. But why would anyone be interested in the *Clicker*? It didn't make sense.

KRISTA

Krista Artino pushed her motorbike to pass the minivan in front of her on the highway. She was a little late to her pole-vaulting practice, and she didn't want to incur the wrath of their coach. Krista had picked up pole-vaulting from her high school track and field days. While she wasn't vying for the Olympics, she was competitive enough to keep up with the rest of the team. She liked the uniqueness of the hobby, but the main attraction was soaring through the air, weightless, adrenaline surging through her body, far from the ground. There wasn't another feeling quite like it.

She pulled into the parking lot with a minute to spare. Just as she pulled off her helmet, her phone rang with an unknown caller. She threw her bag over one shoulder and answered the phone while walking swiftly to the doors.

"Yes?"

"Is this Krista Artino?" a man's deep voice asked in a hesitant tone. She frowned.

"Who is this?"

"Krista, it's Matt Nielsen. I have to tell you something."

"Matt?" Krista nearly stopped in shock, but she remembered the time and keep her feet moving. "How did you get my number? Why are you calling me?"

"Erika gave it to me." Krista had been friends with Matt's sister Erika in high school. While the women didn't see each other much these days, Krista called her every few months for a catch-up. "It's about the fish. And your brother."

This time, Krista did stop. She gripped the phone.

"I'm listening."

"Two guys came to my house a couple of days ago," Matt said in a rush. "They barged in, beat me up. In front of Bianca, too." This last was said in a disgusted, shamed tone. It was obviously a sore point. Krista wondered if he was worried about Bianca's safety, or about looking weak in front of her. Krista had a shrewd guess about which.

"Weird. Terrible. Why?"

"They wanted to know about Sea Salt."

"Is that what you called the drug you developed from that unicorn fish?" Krista snorted. "Lame. So? What did you tell them? What does this have to do with Zeb?"

"They got everything," Matt rasped out. "They were beating me up, Bianca was screaming, I had to tell them. They were really interested in why you kept following me in the *Clicker*, why Zeb was so interested. I think they're after him next."

Krista's stomach clenched in dread.

"What do they want?"

"Information about the drug? I don't know, they must want to use it for something. Wait, you don't know." Matt took a breath. "When I took Sea Salt then jumped in the ocean, it was amazing. No more hallucinations. I got so strong, like I could have swum between islands, fast and far. It was incredible."

"And these guys knew this, somehow?"

"I told a buddy of mine," Matt said quietly. "He's not great at keeping secrets. Word must have got out."

Krista breathed out slowly, trying to rein in her rising temper and fear.

"What exactly did you tell them about Zeb?"

"His interest, how he seemed to know something. The name of the *Clicker*."

"You're a bastard," she spat out, then she sighed. "But you called, so that's something. Who are these people?"

"They wrote their name and phone number on the fridge with a pen, in case I remembered anything else. Bianca cleaned it off before I could memorize the number. She was so mad and afraid."

"You remember the name, at least?"

"I think they called themselves Tangled Net. It was something weird like that. I don't know what it is." Matt paused, then said, "Bianca's coming, I have to go."

The line went dead. Krista cursed and mashed the phone between her hands in frustration. If it wasn't one thing, it was another, with Zeb. She quickly dialed his number to warn him, but it went straight to voicemail. She left a terse message.

She tried Jules next, but it was the same thing. They were probably out of cell range. Who else might he have contact with? Jules was on the boat, and he didn't have any other real friends or family besides herself and Jules.

Corrie might be in contact with him, because of the unicorn fish analysis. Luckily, Krista had her number in her phone, entered earlier in case of emergencies while on the boat. She dialed it.

"Hello?" Corrie's cheery voice answered.

"Corrie, it's Krista Artino." Krista cut through Corrie's immediate greeting and said, "Have you heard from Zeb lately?"

"No, not for a few days. Why?"

"If you get a hold of him, tell him some goons from an organization called Tangled Net are after him. They beat up Matt Nielsen to get information about the drug made from the unicorn fish, which apparently also enhances speed and strength when in the water. I need to warn Zeb, but he's not answering his phone."

"That's crazy," said Corrie. "I'll try him too. You know what, the name Tangled Net rings a bell. I'll look into it."

Krista signed off and leaned against the wall, feeling drained and afraid. Zeb was out on the water, somewhere, in danger. And there was nothing she could do to help.

CORRIE

Corrie hung up from Krista's call, a knot of worry in her stomach. Things had become serious with this unicorn fish, even before now. Their confrontations with Matt were never friendly. But it sounded like Matt was a small player in a dangerous game. Were Zeb and Jules in danger out there on the water? Could these goons find them? What would they do if they did?

Corrie twisted a pipette between her hands. When she noticed what she was doing, she placed it carefully on the counter. Her supervisor wouldn't take kindly to lab equipment broken from her thinking too much. Luckily, no one was here to notice, since it was late on a Friday. She had done enough for today. It was time to pack up, especially if she was going to wreck pipettes instead of being productive.

She hung up her lab coat and walked to her bike, thinking all the way there. Krista had said the goons called themselves Tangled Net. Why did that sound familiar? Corrie searched her mind but couldn't recall where she had heard it. Had a friend mentioned it? Was it a funding agency? Had her mother told her about it?

She hunted through her memories while she coasted down the road to her house but gave up when nothing emerged. Worry for Zeb and Jules surfaced in her mind. There was no way they could be found out on the water, surely. Word of mouth was the only way they could be traced.

Her assurances didn't comfort her.

When she walked in the door, Adrianna came to the top of the stairs.

"Good, you're finally home." She gestured for Corrie to come upstairs.

"What's up?"

Adrianna waited until Corrie was at the top. She looked

excited and brandished her phone in one hand.

"Patrick wrote. Miles Callahan—you know, Patrick's boss, the one with the island—he invited us for lunch tomorrow."

"Oh wow, that's great." Corrie felt a twinge of jealousy that Adrianna would see the exotic fish again. "Take some pictures of the aquarium for me, if you're allowed."

"No, no," said Adrianna. "We're invited. Patrick, me, and you. Miles asked specifically if you were free."

"Me?" Corrie was taken aback. From a brief mention by Adrianna to a personal invite? She didn't know whether to be flattered or alarmed. "What did you tell him about me, that he wants me along?"

"Everything good," Adrianna assured her. "Maybe he sensed a kindred spirit from my description of your interests, I don't know. It's a bit weird, but he's great. The food will be amazing, I promise, and you won't want to miss the aquarium. Just don't tell Hot Lips where you're going."

Corrie laughed. Well, why not go to a private island for lunch and a personal tour of a home aquarium? It was Saturday tomorrow, and she'd been working hard this past week. There was nothing that couldn't wait in the lab. A stab of worry lanced through her at the thought of Zeb and Jules at the mercy of the goons, but she pushed the thought aside. There was no way they would be found on the boat. They were as safe as they could be, and there wasn't anything Corrie could do to help from here.

"I'll probably have to get Hot Lips a bigger tank after seeing whatever Miles has for his fish."

"You'll come?"

"Yes, it sounds like fun. I'm free, and I'm curious about this aquarium." Corrie paused then asked the question that she knew Adrianna wanted to answer. "What should I wear?"

Adrianna's eyes lit up with enthusiasm, as Corrie knew they would.

"Let me help. Lead me to your closet."

KRISTA

Krista stood at the photocopier, waiting for her stack of documents to run through the machine. She hated photocopying. Not only was it exceedingly dull and unbillable grunt work—the paralegals should be doing it, but it was so late that they had already gone home—but it allowed her mind to wander. Krista liked being focused, liked her mind occupied, liked being busy. The mindlessness of photocopying allowed her to think too much. In her present state of mind, that wasn't good.

Zeb was foremost in her thoughts. She wondered where on the coast he was, and a flash of irritation coursed through her. Would it have killed him to let his sister know where he was headed? She was his only family, after all. It was simple courtesy. He was such a stubborn ass sometimes.

Maybe she should find the *Clicker* herself and warn Zeb. She dismissed the notion as folly as soon as she thought it. Without a good reason, there was no way she could take time off work right now. She was already behind because of her week on the boat, and there were multiple deadlines approaching. Her bosses were breathing down her neck, and she needed to make a good impression if she ever wanted to rise in this firm. Anyway, how would she find one small fishing boat in the ocean?

Surely, if the goons had found Zeb, he or Jules would have contacted her. But, again, there was no way the goons could find the *Clicker*. The ocean was a big place, and there were hundreds of harbors and inlets to get lost in. Either way, it wouldn't be an easy task to find them.

Despite this, Krista couldn't help imagining Zeb tied up against the bulwark, fists smashing into his face, his gut. A muscle-bound man slowly snapping his fingers one by one, Zeb screaming at each broken bone. In her mind, his voice sounded like his cries as a child. Jules lying helpless, unconscious on the deck. Zeb's feet tied to a rock, the man heaving Zeb overboard. His screams drowned by the rush of water into his open mouth…

"Photocopying is the worst, isn't it?"

A voice jolted Krista out of her unpleasant reverie, and she jumped.

"Sorry, I didn't mean to startle you." A petite woman with dark hair and large eyes gave her a smile from perfectly rouged lips. Fiona Sullivan was a junior partner and had been at the firm a few years longer than Krista. The word around the office was that she would be promoted shortly. She was good at her job—Krista had seen her in action and had been impressed, and she wasn't impressed easily—but she was the chattiest, most syrupy woman Krista had ever had the misfortune of meeting. She could turn it off for meetings at work—Krista doubted that the men in the firm would take her seriously if she used that voice for work purposes—but it seemed to be her default setting, and she didn't hesitate to use it on colleagues that she felt friendly with. Krista, oddly, seemed to qualify, although she'd given Fiona no reason to be friendly.

"No, it's fine," Krista said. "The photocopier puts me into a daze."

"Oh, I know. It lulls you into false complacency, and then bam! It dies on you, and you spend the next hour on the phone with the support team." Fiona laughed, a rich chuckle that sounded like caramel on her sugary voice. Krista hated desserts.

Krista tried to muster a smile in answer, but it emerged as a grimace. She turned to face the photocopier again in the hope that Fiona would leave her alone to her morose thoughts. Fiona didn't seem to notice.

"Did you hear about Michael and the articled student?" Fiona said, leaning against the wall for comfort. Krista sighed under her breath and didn't respond. Fiona was undeterred.

"Tess saw them in the janitor's closet. You can guess what they were doing. Can you imagine? So much for Michael's attempt at stuffy dignity. We know better. Really, he was hard to take seriously before. You didn't hear it from me, though."

"Michael's extracurricular activities don't concern me," Krista said stiffly. She willed the photocopier to work faster, but it was relentless in its measured pace. She detested office gossip and office politics. She didn't care enough about her colleagues to gossip about them, and she didn't know how to work the system to her advantage or rub elbows with the right people. She put in her hard work and trusted that it would pay off. It mostly did, although sometimes she wondered where she would be if she could pull off both talents. It felt like a level that she didn't want to stoop to.

"Oh, Krista." Fiona chuckled. "Such a good girl. Careful keeping those walls up too high, honey. You have to know what the competition is up to. Never know when you'll need some ammunition."

The photocopier finally, mercifully, completed its job. Krista gathered her papers and fled the supply room with a murmured goodbye. She desperately wanted to tell Fiona where to stuff her gossipy, smarmy ways, but even Krista knew that she had to get along with her colleagues. It wasn't an easy lesson for her to learn—terse words were so much cleaner— but she was trying. Bottling up her retorts made her feel like a volcano about to erupt, but letting loose in the office wouldn't do her any favors.

Krista almost bumped into a suited man entering the supply room.

"In a hurry?" he said. Krista nodded.

"Lots to do, you know the drill."

"Do I ever," he said with a laugh and disappeared into the room.

Krista straightened her papers but was startled by an exclamation of delight from Fiona. She paused to listen, curious despite herself about what had prompted the sound.

"Brilliant." Fiona's voice drifted clearly through the open doorway. "I'll call her right away. You always pull through, Feng. She's a promising contact, since there are whispers about my new case. I've heard that Miles Callahan, the owner of that tech magazine *Tomorrow* and all-around Mr. Moneybags, is into something shady. I don't have details yet, but I sense something juicy coming my way."

"Maybe you should have been a journalist instead of a lawyer," said Feng in a teasing tone. Fiona laughed.

"Yes, so true. I would have been above the fold in the tabloids every week. But the resources here are so much better."

Krista frowned. What would Fiona possibly uncover through gossiping that she couldn't through research in the office?

"Krista."

She jumped and turned. One of the senior partners frowned at her. "Have you finished with the Lombardi case yet?"

"Not quite, but it's coming along."

"I need it done now, Krista. Get on it, please."

Krista swallowed her retort and hurried to her desk. This would be a long night.

CORRIE

Corrie held onto the seat of the zodiac, thrilled at the speed of the orange inflatable boat. Adrianna sat in front of her with Patrick, a hooded jacket protecting her hair from the wind. Corrie let hers blow free. It would look like a mess when they arrived, she was sure, but she couldn't muster up concern through the pleasure of wind on her face.

The zodiac was driven by a groundskeeper. When they had arrived at the dock, north of Victoria, they had been told that Miles was waiting for them on the island. It was just as well, since there was no way to talk without shouting as the boat crashed over waves with stomach-dropping bounces.

They zipped around the network of larger islands until a tiny one peeked out. It was forested, but a rocky beach nestled in the curve of land with a small dock that jutted out from shore. They didn't stop there, but instead circled around the island.

When Corrie saw the other side, it was clear why they were headed there. A massive, multi-tined floating dock thrust out from the cliffside. There was a large powerboat, a catamaran sailboat, numerous kayaks, and another zodiac. Snaking up the cliff was a wide staircase with large landings that contained planters and were ideal for stopping and taking in the view.

Corrie whistled, and Adrianna looked over her shoulder.

"Told you," she shouted. The boat's roar reduced to a dull rumble, and they approached the dock at a stately pace.

At the top of the cliff was a huge house. The entire front was covered in windows, with a lofty wood-beam ceiling visible through the panes from their angle. An expansive patio edged the cliff, and Corrie couldn't wait to climb up there and look around for herself.

A man stood on the patio. When he saw them look up, he waved.

"There's Miles," Adrianna said. "What do you think?"

"Incredible," said Corrie. "You have friends in the right places."

"That's Addy," said Patrick with a laugh. "Always making friends. I don't know if I would have been invited back by myself."

"Don't sell yourself short," Adrianna said. "He likes you. He was even talking about a promotion."

"I don't want to count my chickens before they've hatched," Patrick said, but he looked content.

Miles walked with quick steps down the stairs while they meandered into a free space at the dock. When they pulled up and bumped gently into place, he was there to grab the painter.

"Welcome to Kurina Island," Miles said. His voice was rich and tuneful, and Corrie liked it at once. He tied the painter to a cleat and held out his hand. "You must be Corrie Duval. It's a pleasure to meet you."

Corrie took his hand and let him help her out of the boat. She tried to run her fingers through her hair to smooth it but gave up the impossible task immediately.

"You too, Mr. Callahan."

"Please, call me Miles." He turned to help Adrianna out of the boat. She smoothed her skirt and gave Miles a beam.

"Thank you for the invite, Miles. I was dying to see your place again. It's stunning."

Miles laughed. The richness reminded Corrie of chocolate. It matched his styled dark hair and charming smile perfectly.

"It's wonderful to have you here. I love coming to Kurina Island, but it lacks a certain *je ne sais quoi* without engaging company."

"It must be so difficult, having a beautiful private island," Corrie said with a tease in her voice. She was testing his reaction to see what sort of person he was, and how she should tailor their conversation to suit. To her satisfaction, he laughed.

"You're quite right, I shouldn't be asking for sympathy, should I?" He offered Corrie his arm and she took it with a smile. "Please, come up to the patio and help a poor man enjoy this place."

"What a gentleman," she said as they walked toward the stairs. "I feel like I should be wearing a large hat with imitation grapes on it."

"Ostrich feathers are quite *de rigueur*, I've been told," he said in the same teasing tone.

"Well, we must bow to fashion, mustn't we?"

They chatted in this manner until the top of the stairs. Corrie looked at the surroundings and whistled.

"Quite the place you have here. Tell me about it. The name, first. What does 'Kurina' mean?" She wanted to give him an opportunity to boast. It would make him happy and give her something to talk about.

"I'm glad you asked." Miles looked pleased. "It's short for *Mitsukurina owstoni*, the deep-sea goblin shark."

Corrie nodded in recognition.

"The living fossil with the long snout and that crazy extendible jaw. Why that one?"

"I adore all things rare and exotic," Miles said. "The goblin shark certainly qualifies."

"I like it." Corrie smiled at him. That was just the sort of name she would choose, if she had her own private island. Her admiration for Miles intensified. She swept her arm around the top of the cliff. "Tell me what you have here."

"That's the pool house." Miles pointed to a large structure with two walls made entirely of windows. Inside, a kidney bean-shaped pool was half-covered in blue tiles. The other half was torn up, and the pool was empty. "We're redoing the tiling, otherwise I would have told you to bring swimsuits. Bad timing."

"Can't have everything, I suppose," Corrie said with a wink. "Now we can only have lunch on a beautiful patio with an amazing view. What a letdown."

Miles laughed.

"The guest cottage is down there." He pointed past the pool house. "And the path to the beach. No white sands here, but it's pretty, all the same. Oh, look, Bertrand is out." He pointed at an albino peacock who had strutted out from behind a tree. "I have a white peahen named Gertrude, as well. Quite a glorious pair, but Bertie has the magnificent tail. And there's the main house, of course."

Adrianna and Patrick joined them.

"I know that one," said Adrianna. "You will show Corrie the aquarium, won't you, Miles?"

"I'm dying to see it," said Corrie.

"Absolutely," Miles said with a good-natured smile. "But might I suggest we have our lunch, first? My chef has it prepared already, and I don't like to keep good food waiting."

"No, definitely not," said Corrie. "That would be a tragedy. I'm sure the fish will be there once we're done."

They followed Miles to the patio, whose cedar expanse could easily seat forty. Instead, a cozy table for four was pushed close to the railing and surrounded by cushioned wrought-iron chairs. Plates of sandwiches on delicious-looking breads, bowls of salads, platters of crab cakes, and other delectable finger foods were clustered in the center of the table. Miles pulled out a chair for Corrie, and Patrick did the same for Adrianna after she nudged him.

When they were seated, Miles pulled out a bottle of wine that was chilling in a metal vessel filled with crushed ice.

"Wine, Corrie? It's a sauvignon blanc from Southern France, nineteen seventy-three. There were only thirty bottles produced, and I bought most of them. It's dry, with a fruity finish of melons."

"How can I say no to melons?" Corrie held out her wine glass with a laugh. "Don't pour much, I'm afraid it will be wasted on me. You obviously have a refined palate for wine."

"I like finding the novel in any situation," he said with an agreeable smile. "But never say wine is wasted. I enjoy letting you discover your own palate. Wine, Adrianna?"

They passed the lunch in pleasant conversation. Miles was engaging, quick-witted, and easy to talk to. Corrie found herself liking him more and more. He was very interested in her work, and they spent ten solid minutes discussing the finer points of anemone collection, and another ten on the greater ramifications of the cancer-fighting metabolites that her bacteria produced. The food was excellent, and although Corrie knew very little about fine wine, the glass she had went down very easily.

Once they had all eaten enough and had finished their last sips of wine, Miles put his hands on the table.

"Now that we are fed and watered, are you still interested in viewing the aquarium?"

"Yes, of course." Corrie stood quickly. "I have a fish tank at home, with a pleco named Hot Lips in it. I'd like to see what the grown-up version looks like."

"More water, bigger fish," Miles said with a chuckle. "But, in essence, similar. It's inside the house, this way."

He led them to glass doors that were flung open to the warm spring air. Inside, the open-concept room was huge, and dotted with tastefully chosen chairs and couches arranged to admire the view. Miles bypassed all these and headed straight to a pair of double doors on the side. They were translucent, with kelp and sea lions sandblasted into the glass. Miles pushed both doors open for effect, and Corrie gasped.

"Wow," she breathed. "Hot Lips would be so jealous."

Adrianna gave an amused giggle.

"Told you it was great," she said. "Check out the sharks."

Corrie didn't know where to look first. There were seven tanks in total. Four were inset into the walls at eye height and were the size of large coolers, two were cylindrical tubes stretching from floor to ceiling, and one spanned the entire back wall. Corrie wanted to do each tank justice, so she started with the smaller ones. One held a variety of jellyfish-like creatures.

"What's this one?" Corrie asked, pointing at a translucent, rose-colored animal in mid-water. It had a strange mouth in its center. "It looks like an echinoderm, but I don't recognize it."

"Good eye." Miles sounded pleased. "It's a Pink Sea-through Fantasia, a free-swimming sea cucumber. It was only recently discovered in the western Pacific Ocean."

Corrie moved to the next tank. It was barely lit, but inside she could make out a crustacean the size of her head and a creature with eight arms and two ear-like fins.

"Is that a deep-sea dumbo squid? And what's the crustacean?"

"It's a giant isopod. They're not rare, and even some public aquariums have them, but I couldn't resist getting it to keep my squid company, since they're both from the deep-sea. Most of the tanks have their own separate systems, because the fish are from different environments and need different conditions."

Corrie moved to the cylindrical tanks. The fish in one of them made her start backward.

"You have a coelacanth?" she screeched. The reptilian fish with thick fins was only recently discovered, and it was virtually unchanged from when the dinosaurs roamed. It was like looking at a fossil. She'd only ever seen pictures before. "Alive?"

"So far," Miles said. He seemed pleased at her reaction. "It was a devil to get here. I had to ship it from Madagascar."

Corrie didn't know what to think. Miles had gone to such lengths to collect these fish, and for what? To occasionally look at them in his aquarium? She didn't understand the impulse. The only commonality between the creatures was that they were rare and very hard to get.

She shook her head in amazement and turned to the largest tank. It was stunning, filled with realistic-looking rock formations covered with anemones and sea stars. Five small sharks circled inside.

"Australian ghost shark, frilled shark, birdbeak dogfish, and striped catshark," Miles said. "Frilled sharks are particularly difficult to catch, so that was a real find. Not all of them are rare, but they look good together in my collection."

"What's that one?" Corrie pointed at the shark Miles hadn't named. It was small and had numerous dark patches on its top side. She didn't recognize it.

"I was hoping you might know," Miles said. "But I guess I'll have to call in my aquatics expert to identify it. I only got it a week ago, from local waters, too. I can't find it in any of the books. I don't know if it's a new species, or a rare variety of a common shark. Either way, it fits perfectly in my collection."

Corrie held her breath and put her face as close to the tank as she could without smudging the glass. What was it? It looked like a shark, but the dorsal fin had a strange hook on the top, and there were deep cuts in each pectoral fin, the purpose of which Corrie couldn't guess.

Her heart started to beat wildly. Miles had found a new species, at the same time as she and Zeb had found the unicorn fish and Sucker. What were the odds that they were connected? Pretty high, she had no doubt. Here was another unusual creature, and Miles had it in his keeping. She tried to contain her excitement, but her leg jiggled under her sundress.

"I don't know what it is, but it's fascinating," she said in a neutral voice. "I'd love a blood sample for testing."

Miles nodded.

"And you shall have it, my lady," he said. "When my expert comes, I'll get him to draw one for you."

"That would be amazing."

Miles spread his hands.

"That's the tour," he said. "Ladies, if you'll excuse us, I need to speak to Patrick for a moment about work. Feel free to look at the fish more or retire to the patio."

ADRIANNA

Miles led Patrick out of the aquarium room. Patrick looked surprised and pleased that Miles wanted to talk about work. Adrianna hoped for his sake that it was good news. Patrick had been angling for an early promotion, since he had been hired at a lower level than his skill set called for. Since Miles was taking an interest in him, Adrianna was hopeful that today was the day.

There wasn't anything Adrianna could do to help Patrick, so she turned to Corrie.

"Pretty amazing, right?" She waved at the tanks full of exotic sea creatures. "It's quite a collection."

"Yeah," Corrie said slowly.

"I thought you'd like it," Adrianna pressed further.

"Yeah," Corrie repeated. She stared intently into the large tank at one of the sharks swimming in circles.

"Purple monkey dishwasher," Adrianna said. Corrie finally shook herself out of her preoccupation and looked at Adrianna in puzzlement.

"Dishwasher?" she said. "What are you talking about?"

"Just seeing if you were listening. What's up? I know you like fish, but your level of distraction is more than I expected."

"Do you know what kind of shark that is?" Corrie pointed at the spotted one that she and Miles had been talking about earlier. Adrianna shook her head.

"No. You're the biologist. How do you expect me to know if you don't? I know Jaws, and that's about it."

Corrie hesitated. Then she looked right into Adrianna's eyes. Adrianna was startled to see Corrie's intensity. She was usually bubbly and cheerful. This was strange.

"It's not normal," she whispered. "I know it's not. Can you keep a secret? Please?"

Adrianna frowned. What was going on? Corrie was lovely,

but she never appeared to have hidden depths. What had her friend been hiding from her?

"What is it?"

"Please promise. It's important."

"As long as it's not illegal or something," Adrianna joked. Corrie shook her head without smiling.

"Nothing like that. Promise?"

Adrianna finally relented. She couldn't not know Corrie's secret now. She was obligated to agree.

"I promise."

Corrie pulled her to a corner of the room, away from the door, and spoke quickly in a whisper.

"I didn't tell you everything about the boat. Zeb and I found a fish, one that's totally different from all other known fish. We're talking new species discovery. I even checked its genetic makeup, and it's clearly a separate species. And then—" Corrie gulped, and her eyes grew wide. Adrianna leaned closer to catch every word. "There was a giant octopus that followed us. It was huge, Adrianna, insanely huge. Bigger than the boat huge. It wasn't anything I knew. And now this shark—something's going on, and I don't know what it is. Were these fish hiding somewhere and were suddenly released? Was there an episode of rapid evolution, maybe from radiation poisoning?"

"That wouldn't happen so neatly," Adrianna said automatically. She tried to process Corrie's words. Three new species discovered on this coast? She could imagine one, maybe, but not three in a few weeks. She attempted to inject some rationality into the conversation.

"Are you sure you weren't mistaken? Maybe the fish you found was different—mutation, maybe—but this shark could have been undiscovered. I mean, look at it. It mostly looks like the other sharks. And the giant octopus." Adrianna tried to look understanding. "Were you taking something? Drinking too much, maybe a bit of weed? Something stronger? I won't judge, I promise.”

“No!” Corrie hissed vehemently. “Nothing, I swear. It was as real as you or me.”

Adrianna let out a long sigh. Corrie was asking her to accept something unbelievable. When was the last time a new fish species had been discovered on the coast? Decades, at the very least. And an octopus the size of a boat?

But Corrie was a scientist. She lived by data and facts. Her philosophy was necessarily tempered by the scientific method—observations, hypotheses, testing—and Adrianna couldn’t believe Corrie would take a flight of fancy without considering her observations very carefully.

But, above all, Corrie was her friend. If she said that she’d found a flying pig, Adrianna would buy extra barbeque sauce. Adrianna took her friendship duties very seriously. If Corrie needed her to believe in giant octopuses, then Adrianna could try her best to do so.

Corrie stared at her nervously. Adrianna touched her shoulder in reassurance.

“Okay,” she said. “I believe you. What do you want me to do?”

Corrie sagged in relief.

“Nothing,” she said. “You don’t have to do anything. I just wanted someone to know, someone other than me. Someone to talk to about it.”

Adrianna put her arm around Corrie’s shoulders.

“I can do that.”

ZEBALLOS

Zeb was underwater, searching for the creatures that he now despaired of ever seeing again. For days now, he had seen nothing but lingcod and perch and all the useless fish that he'd known all his life. Where were the creatures from his mother's stories? Where were the strolias, the krolls, and the others that he hadn't yet seen but knew must exist, if strolias and krolls and brigars did? It didn't make sense. Why would he see so many before, and now nothing?

He opened his fist and held out a piece of dried jellyfish. The strolia they had captured had liked it. Maybe he could entice one to him if they caught the scent. It was a feeble hope, he knew, but he was running out of options. He had been searching all week with no success, and Krista's voice was loud in his head, yelling about the cost of running the boat with no paying customers. He tried to ignore it, but his sister was persistent, even when she was imaginary.

A live jellyfish floated by his hand, and Zeb reached out and grabbed it. It was firm between his fingers, despite its squishy appearance. His mouth watered. He tried to disregard it—he'd tried fresh jellyfish before, and it didn't satisfy like the dried stuff briefly did, and it sometimes stung his mouth on the way down—but he couldn't stop his hand from bringing it to his mouth. His fingers pushed the whole jellyfish inside, and he chewed and swallowed, feeling both revulsion and a terrible hunger.

As he suspected, it did nothing to quench the need. His body grumbled in dissatisfaction, but he didn't know how to please it. He would simply have to ignore it, as he usually did.

He shoved the dried jellyfish into his mouth in exasperation—it clearly wasn't summoning any strolias, so he might as well wash down the live jellyfish with something better—and decided to use the last of his current breath to enjoy himself. He struck out with flippered feet to the seafloor, exploring rock formations and colorful anemones the size of his head. Being underwater felt more comfortable than air some days.

It was never like this before. Swimming was always fun, but it was never a need. He remembered his mother disappearing for a whole day at a time near the end. Had she felt the same way? There was so much he didn't know, and so much he couldn't remember. He wished he could have known her for longer, and a familiar ache settled beside the hunger in his stomach.

When he climbed aboard, Jules had lunch ready for him. Once again, Jules had put a few pieces of jellyfish on his plate without comment. Zeb stared at them for a moment, hating that he needed them, hating that they did so little to dull the hunger, and feeling grateful to Jules for sticking beside him on this fruitless journey.

"Hope you didn't need to look anything up," Jules said through a mouthful of sandwich. "We're out of cell range again. Coverage is terrible on this coast."

Zeb pulled out his phone. Sure enough, the reception was down to zero. The screen indicated that he had a voicemail from Krista, but there was no way he could check it now.

"Krista called," he said. "Hope it wasn't urgent. It'll have to wait, now."

JULES

Jules was searching for pasta. He was certain they still had a bag of rigatoni left on board, but he couldn't find it.

"The galley's not that big," he grumbled to himself. He pushed aside cans of tomato paste and chickpeas in a top cupboard, and his eyes fruitlessly raked across the otherwise empty space. He stepped back and looked around the tiny area with a frown. There wasn't anywhere else to look.

His eye caught a bottom cupboard door that was tucked around the corner.

"There you are, you sneaky bugger," Jules said. He knelt and opened the door then rummaged inside the low area. His fingers grasped crinkly plastic, but when he pulled it out, it was only a bag of dried mangoes. He bent over to get a good look.

"Yes," Jules breathed. A bag of pasta squatted in the back of the deep cupboard. He reached out and picked it up. His glance fell upon the switch that didn't do anything that he had found last week. Once again, he wondered why anyone would install a switch in a deep cupboard that turned nothing on.

"Hey, Zeb!" Jules shouted. "Come here."

When Zeb wandered in, Jules motioned him to kneel on the floor.

"Come on, have a look at this."

"If you've found a rat in the galley, I'm not interested."

"Just get down here."

Zeb crouched and stuck his head into the narrow space.

"What's that switch for?" Jules asked. "Do you know? I've flicked it on and off a few times, but nothing happens. It's a pretty dumb spot to have a switch, if you ask me."

Zeb pulled his head out of the cupboard and looked pensive.

"Not if you want to keep it a secret. Who would look for it there, unless they knew about it?"

"But it doesn't do anything," Jules repeated. Zeb reached in and flicked the switch a few times experimentally. Nothing happened. Jules shrugged. "Told you."

Zeb stared at Jules for a moment. Understanding lit his eyes, and he jumped up. Jules fell back on his hands in startlement.

"Give me one minute," Zeb said. He stripped off his shirt and dropped it on the floor as he backed out of the galley. "Then turn the switch on for one minute, then off again, one minute each time. Okay?"

"What do you think it is?" Jules called after Zeb, but he was already hopping out of his pants down the hall toward the outer door. Jules shook his head in resignation. "It would have taken him two more seconds to tell me."

He checked the galley clock and waited a minute after he heard a splash, then he flicked the switch on. He waited for a few seconds then jumped up and ran water from the tap into a saucepan. He might as well start cooking his pasta while Zeb was testing whatever he was testing.

After a few minutes of flicking the switch off and on, the sound of footsteps on the deck alerted Jules to Zeb's presence. A moment later, Zeb stood dripping in the doorway. Jules waved at him.

"At the risk of sounding like Krista, you're getting water all over the floor. Get a towel."

"It will dry. Come out, I need you to look at something."

"But my water is almost boiling."

"Turn it off for now, we'll eat later."

Jules grunted—Zeb didn't understand the importance of timing in cooking—but since nothing was waiting on his pasta to cook, he would let it slide. Zeb practically buzzed with restrained excitement, and Jules was genuinely curious what he'd found. He followed Zeb to the deck.

"There's a device attached to the hull," Zeb said when they were outside. "I saw it last week, but I didn't know what it was, and I forgot to look in the boat because we found Sucker shortly after."

"It was a rather momentous week," Jules agreed.

"It gives off a weird noise, kind of a deep sonar boop."

"A boop," Jules repeated in a neutral tone. Zeb rolled his eyes.

"I don't know, that's what it sounds like. That switch, though, it turns the noise on and off. What is it, and why is the switch hidden?" Zeb's jaw tightened. "Just another secret of George Artino. I want you to come and have a look at it. It's stuck on the hull really well—it might be welded on there—but I could use another pair of eyes."

Jules appreciated Zeb's desire for his opinion—not many people wanted it, usually—but he looked dubiously at the water.

"I try not to immerse myself in water one degree up from iceberg formation," he said. "I know you're immune, but the rest of us are susceptible to a little thing known as hypothermia."

"Use my wetsuit. It'll only be for a minute. I need to find out what this thing is."

Zeb looked at him with pleading eyes, and Jules gave a deep sigh.

"Fine. But you're making the spiked hot chocolate when I get out."

"Done."

Zeb raced to get his wetsuit, and Jules plodded to find his swim shorts. He emerged a minute later, shivering and grumbling under his breath. Zeb held out the wetsuit.

"This is going to be too loose," Jules said as he stepped into the leg holes. "You have muscles from swimming, and I like to think of myself as lean and toned."

Zeb squeezed Jules' bicep with a grin, and Jules elbowed him out of the way.

"Careful," Jules said. "I'm getting in this ice bath out of the generosity of my heart."

The wetsuit was baggy in the chest, as Jules had expected,

and he braced himself for the rush of cold water when he climbed down the ladder to the sloshing waves below. It was worse than he had expected, and it took his breath away.

"See, it's not that bad," Zeb said. He treaded water beside the ladder. Jules grimaced at him.

"It's worse, iceman. Far worse." Jules adjusted his mask and released his breath to psych himself up for the plunge. "Come on, let's get this over with."

Jules let himself fall backward and the sea closed over his head. Icy water gushed down his back and his shoulders shrank on themselves in an instinctual attempt to reduce surface area. It didn't work.

He burst to the surface and heaved a gulp of air, then he cursed loudly and eloquently. Zeb bobbed next to him.

"Are you done?" Zeb said when Jules had finished shouting his displeasure. "The sooner we check it out, the sooner you can get on board."

Jules spluttered with indignation, but Zeb only grinned and descended out of sight. Jules took a deep breath and followed.

Jules was an indifferent swimmer—a few lessons as a child had garnished his summertime lake excursions with enough skill to keep him from drowning—but he never worried if Zeb was nearby. His friend's extraordinary abilities would be enough to keep Jules out of trouble, should the need arise.

Jules followed Zeb's red flippered feet alongside the hull of the *Clicker*. Under the waves it was calmer than the sloshing surface, and the green algae cast a strange light over everything. Jules looked at his hands. His already pale fingers looked sickly and gangrenous, and he reminded himself never to go swimming with an attractive woman. The thought made him laugh, and he almost gulped a mouthful of seawater. He rose to the surface and heaved another breath before diving down once more. He cursed the need for movement, since every time he twisted or kicked, frigid water poured into his ill-fitting suit.

Zeb waved him forward, and Jules gave him the finger before he joined him at the boat. He looked closer.

There was a device attached to the vessel. It sat inert on the metal hull, streamlined and covered in an opaque shell. It was no wider than his outstretched fingers and jutted out half as high from the hull. Jules took a quick look then escaped to the surface for a breath of air. When he returned, Zeb floated next to the device with a questioning look in his unmasked eyes.

Jules touched the device, trying to find any crack that he could slip a fingernail or a crowbar into, but the device was fastened to the hull with a tough adhesive and plenty of sealant. After a few seconds of examination, Jules turned to Zeb and gave him an exaggerated shrug.

But Zeb wasn't looking at him. His gaze was over Jules' shoulder, and his wide eyes were partly fearful, partly awestruck. Jules twisted around to look and winced at the rush of cold water down his back.

One glance, and he forgot his coldness. A school of unicorn fish, Zeb's strolias, swam by, their scales glimmering with iridescent rainbows that dazzled his eyes. Zeb gripped his forearm tightly, and when Jules looked at him, his face was open and excited, wonder filling it. Jules didn't remember ever seeing him show that much visible emotion about anything before.

Zeb's fingers tightened until their vise-like grip pinched. Jules moved to swat him away, but a motion caught his peripheral vision. He turned to look.

On the edge of their visibility through the murky algae, something massive glided. Jules couldn't see a head nor a tail, only a long, constantly moving, sinuous body gliding in and out of his vision. Dark green scales lay smoothly on a cylindrical form that was as wide as Jules was tall.

Jules froze for a long moment, only able to see the massive creature, not able to process it. Then his brain kicked into flight mode. He tore away from Zeb's grasp and flailed to the surface, his lungs only now remembering to burn from a lack of oxygen. His only coherent thought, swirling in the chaos of his panic, was to get out of the water. The boat might be no better—that eel-like thing was as big as a house, and presumably the *Clicker* was no match for it—but at least he could breathe air before he died.

He thrashed at the surface and gulped a great lungful of air before he struck out for the ladder. His strokes were loose and inefficient, and he despaired of ever reaching the safety of the *Clicker*. His panicked brain threatened to take over, and he choked on a mouthful of seawater.

Damn it, he didn't want to die like this. His life might not matter to anyone else, but it was his to live. Being swallowed by a sea monster was not the way he wanted to go.

Hands grabbed his torso and thrust him up to the light. Jules sputtered and coughed, his legs kicking feebly, but the hands didn't let go. Arms wrapped around his middle and he found himself moving toward the ladder. His body caught up with his brain and he stopped struggling, concentrating instead on breathing, letting Zeb steer him to the boat. When he was close enough, he grasped the rungs of the ladder and hauled himself up to the deck.

Jules couldn't get to his feet, and instead dragged himself to a seated position, leaning against the bulwark. Now that he was out of the water, and his breathing came in less ragged gasps, his body began to shiver violently from the cold and shock. What had they encountered under the waves?

Zeb climbed aboard and crouched next to Jules with a look of concern.

"Are you okay?"

Jules laughed, but it came out as a raspy croak.

"Holy crap, Zeb. What the hell was that? What is going on?" He closed his eyes as his shivering turned to uncontrollable shudders. "I don't know, man, I don't know if I can do this."

Zeb lifted him under the arms and supported him as Jules

stumbled to the cabin.

"Come on," he said. "We need to get you dry. And make that spiked hot chocolate, right?"

Jules' fumbling fingers couldn't grasp the zipper, so Zeb pulled him out of his suit, wrapped him in a towel, then pushed a sweater over his head and helped him find the arm holes. Jules felt like a child, but he was grateful for the help. His body certainly wasn't cooperating enough to aid him sufficiently.

In the eating area, Zeb pushed him firmly onto the bench at the table and moved around the galley to boil water. Jules couldn't tear his eyes away from the waves through the little window next to his head. He kept expecting a dark green hump of sinuous body to crest above the cold ocean surface. His shudders had only reduced to shivers, and he wrapped himself more tightly in the blanket that Zeb had insisted he wear.

A wave hit the boat broadside and rocked the vessel. Jules gasped then felt stupid. It was probably from a passing ferry, but he couldn't stop imagining the creature bumping their hull.

Zeb sat on the bench and slid a mug toward him. Jules gripped it with cold fingers, glad for the heat. They sat in silence until Jules broke it.

"What was that?"

Zeb's mouth twisted in thought.

"If I had to guess, it was a *ligan*. Giant sea serpent," he added, although Jules didn't appreciate the clarification. "Giant sea serpent" was not a phrase he needed rolling around in his head. Zeb continued. "I wondered if it was a whale or something, but it clearly had defined scales, so it has to be fish or reptile. The size of it means it could be a shark, but no shark is that long, and none are that color. It has to be a ligan."

Jules closed his eyes and sipped his hot chocolate, but the images swimming behind his eyelids made him force them open once more.

"Ligan. Good. Now I have a name for the nightmare. That will be helpful tonight."

Zeb grimaced.

"I'm sorry you had to deal with that. I've never seen—well, obviously, it's all new to me, too. My mum said they're not always ferocious predators, though. They can be friendly under the right circumstances."

"Under the right—" Jules took a steadying breath. "You really need to work on your bedside manner. You're not reassuring me at all."

"Sorry." Zeb looked contrite, and they sipped their drinks in silence.

"Could you hear the sonar?" Zeb said finally. Jules shook his head.

"No, not at all."

"Really?" Zeb looked puzzled.

"I wasn't down for that long between breaths, though."

"You would have heard it. It makes that noise often, and it's hard to miss. Why couldn't you hear it?"

"Music too loud in my headphones, maybe. Hearing loss at certain frequencies." Jules sank lower in his seat and half-closed his eyes. That way, he could rest them without seeing the ligan again. "You're weird in other ways, though. Maybe you have better underwater hearing, too."

When Jules glanced at Zeb, he was frowning.

"What does that mean?" he muttered, half to himself.

"Maybe it's calling you and all the other weird fish out there," Jules said. He was mostly joking, but Zeb sat bolt upright.

"Do you think that's what it's doing?" Zeb's eyes were wide.

Jules wasn't sure what Zeb suddenly understood, but Jules hoped he had been able to help, even a little bit. He was pretty useless otherwise, as their excursion has proved.

"Doing what, calling the creatures?"

"Yes, and that's why we didn't see them all this week, because the switch was off. And maybe the switch was on when Corrie was on board, and that's why Sucker was always nearby to sense the strolia slime."

Zeb gripped the table in his excitement. Despite his own fear and discomfort, Jules was happy to see Zeb's animation. He hadn't seen him this excited or lighthearted since his dad had died, or maybe before, since the big fight. Whatever these weird creatures were about, it somehow gave Zeb a purpose. Jules just wished his friend could have found healing from his grief from something other than a giant sea monster.

"I might have toggled the switch around that time," Jules offered.

"I'm going to see if the sonar is on, and if the fish are there," Zeb said. He leaped up.

"Wait," Jules said in panic. "You can't go down. That ligan is still there. You can't…" Jules didn't know what the solution was—never swimming again wasn't an option for Zeb, that was certain—but it terrified Jules to think that Zeb could dive in and be instant fodder for a giant sea serpent. What if Zeb never came up again? What would he tell Krista? What would he do without his best friend?

Some of what he was feeling must have been written on his face, because Zeb put a hand on his shoulder.

"I'll only be two minutes, okay? I promise. At the first sign of the ligan, I'll come back up."

Jules nodded stiffly, and Zeb walked to the door.

"I'm watching the galley clock," Jules shouted after him. Zeb waved to acknowledge the words.

ZEBALLOS

Zeb felt bad leaving a clearly panic-stricken Jules alone on the boat, but it had to be done. He had to find out if the sonar device was attracting creatures from his mother's stories. He didn't have the faintest inkling how that was possible, or why. All he knew was that the creatures were not there, then Jules turned on the switch, and they appeared.

And why couldn't Jules hear the sound? Zeb shivered, but not from cold. He felt close to answers, but they were still obscured by heavy fog. He missed having Corrie on board for her sharp mind. She would have at least three theories immediately upon hearing the news, he had no doubt.

First things first: confirm that the creatures were still nearby when the sonar was on. Zeb climbed down the ladder instead of diving in, mindful of Jules' concern over the ligan. His mother had told him that ligans were huge and deadly, but only to those that threatened them or their friends, for they were intelligent and fiercely loyal. Assuming his mother's stories held enough truth to be useful, he shouldn't have much to worry about—he hoped.

He slipped into the cool water with a deep breath. His shoulders relaxed and he closed his eyes to sense the water around him. There was motion, but it took a moment for him to decipher what it was from. Some smaller fish swam in a school below him, a strange disturbance in front of each fish indicating that they were horned strolias. That answered his question, at least. Zeb's smile was wide.

There was a long, swirling current surrounding the boat, which Zeb didn't understand. He opened his eyes and peered through the murk.

A dark shadow passed close to him. Despite his usual calmness underwater, Zeb flinched. Dark green scales slid by in an endless cycle around their boat. The body flowed past, sometimes too far away to see, sometimes near enough to touch. Zeb swam back to avoid contact with the scales. As tempted as he was to touch physical evidence of a ligan, he couldn't risk it. If his mother hadn't told him the whole story, he wouldn't stand a chance against an angry ligan.

Although he wanted to stay down for longer, his curiosity was satisfied. Mindful of Jules watching the clock, Zeb swam with swift strokes to the ladder and emerged from the sea.

Jules shuffled out of the cabin when Zeb pulled up the ladder with a clang.

"It was two and a half minutes," he said, then tried a weak smile. "Did you see anything?"

Zeb debated internally what to tell Jules and decided on a portion of the truth.

"There was a school of strolias. I'm sure we're right, that the device sends out a signal that the creatures can hear. It must attract them. I don't know why."

"You hear it," Jules said. "What do you hear in it? Does it make you feel frisky or something?"

Zeb snorted.

"Not particularly. I don't notice any draw to it, but then, I'm never far away from the boat."

Jules passed Zeb a towel, and he dried off then led the way into the cabin. Jules still looked too pale and clutched his blanket tightly around him. It didn't feel cold outside to Zeb, but it was cloudy with a decent breeze, so it was probably best to get Jules inside.

Zeb ducked into his cabin to change. When he returned to the galley, Jules had started his pot of water boiling again.

"Hungry yet?" Jules asked him. The blanket was discarded on the bench, and Jules looked calmer in his domain. "I'll start the pasta."

"Sounds good."

"I turned off the switch," Jules said without looking at him. "When I heard you on the ladder. I figured we don't need to attract these creatures to our boat when you're not swimming."

"Yeah, you're right," Zeb said. Jules relaxed his shoulders at Zeb's approval, and Zeb tapped his chin in thought. "I feel like we need to keep track of these creatures, if we're going to see more of them in the future. My mum had a whole slew of stories, only some of which I remember much about. We should have some way to keep them straight."

"Like a logbook, with dates of sightings and notes about what they do," Jules said.

"Exactly. Corrie would be proud of you."

"Her sciencing rubbed off, I guess. Science through osmosis." Jules clapped his hands. "So, what do we have so far?"

Zeb leaned into the table and extracted a pencil and an old notebook with worn corners. He ripped out a few used pages, but most of the book was intact. A thrill of excitement warmed his stomach. Things were really happening, and he and Jules were writing down the evidence to prove it. Maybe, if they figured out what was down there, answers would swirl up from the depths.

"Strolias, aka unicorn fish." Zeb wrote the name at the top of a page then jotted down a few notes below. "Rainbow skin. Single horn coming out of head, poisoned tip. Swims in schools. Makes slime that attracts brigars." Zeb flipped to the next page and wrote at the top. "Brigars, aka Sucker. Giant octopus. What's the word Corrie used for its relationship with the strolias?"

"Symbiotic," Jules said after a pause.

"Right. Symbiotic with strolias. Not to be messed with." Zeb flipped the page again. "Ligan. Giant sea serpent. Loyal to friends, deadly to enemies."

"How do you become a friend?" Jules shuddered. Zeb flipped to the strolia page to distract him from thoughts of the ligan.

"It's a bit empty," he said. "We don't have much." A thought struck him. "Hey, do you think you could sketch each fish? Just a quick one, so we can see them at a glance."

"I hardly saw Sucker and the ligan," Jules said.

"I know, but I could describe them to you. It's just for our book. Come on, I know you still remember art class. It was one of the few you showed up for, after all."

Jules shrugged, but then he waved at Zeb to hand over the notebook.

"Watch my water. Put the pasta in when it boils."

Jules moved to the table and sat. Zeb watched as he started to sketch a strolia. He was tentative at first, but slowly his pencil strokes grew surer. A horned fish emerged from the page, a little cartoonish but correct in essentials. Jules finished and held it at arm's length with a critical eye.

"It looks like it should have a speech bubble," he said. "But that's what you get when you learn to draw from cartoon books in your dad's bookstore."

"It's great," Zeb said, and he meant it. The drawing really brought their impromptu logbook to life. He shivered with excitement, and a rare grin lifted his cheeks. Jules saw the smile.

"You're a lot more expressive underwater, did you know that?"

"What do you mean?" Zeb was confused. He was himself, above or under the waves.

"Just what I said. Your expressions are more exaggerated." Jules corrected himself. "Like, they're more open and normal underwater. You're pretty closed off up here, at least around other people beside me. Maybe you're more comfortable down there, I don't know."

Jules bent to his work. Zeb pondered his words while he gave descriptions of the brigar and ligan to Jules. He did feel freer underwater, more himself, but he hadn't realized it translated into something visible.

CORRIE

It was Monday morning, and Corrie was regretting spending so much time galivanting on the weekend. Not that she hadn't had fun with Miles and the others—visiting a private island was a once-in-a-lifetime experience, and Miles had made it doubly pleasant—but there was so much for her to do in the lab.

She started some chemical reactions for her anemone project. While they were incubating, she printed the read-out from the mass spectrometry machine with her slime protein results. It didn't show her anything new from the other day, but Corrie needed something tangible between her fingers to think properly.

Her fingertip traced the line that showed the amino acid anomaly that the protein contained. Was it a mistake, a malfunction in the machine, or was it the cause of the hallucinations and enhancements? She didn't know enough to answer that. She wasn't a physiologist, or a medical researcher, or even a specialist in studying proteins. She was only a first-year master's student, and she was in over her head.

Corrie wished she hadn't been so rash in putting the unicorn fish they had captured back in the water. She could have taken tissue samples from Spiky and looked at them under the microscope to find out where the protein was being produced. Maybe she could have done tracer studies and protein imaging to follow the protein back to its source in the fish's body. There was so much she could look for…

Corrie shook her head. She was at risk of this project consuming her. She still had her anemones and bacteria to study, and despite the yearnings of her heart, they were more important, if only for providing her a cover for her fish work.

No, she scolded herself. They were important, too. She was contributing to the body of science that would help treat cancer. Was there a loftier goal than that?

New species are earth-shattering, too, her inner voice said. She stood up straight and reached for her lab coat to continue her other work. She couldn't get lost in this.

"Are these data for me to see?" said a voice behind her. Corrie whirled around. While she'd been lost in her thoughts, Jonathan had snuck up. The print-out of the slime protein lay on the bench with nothing else to distract from it. Corrie thought quickly.

"It's a control run," she said. "I messed it up, though, must have contaminated it somehow. I have to re-run it to get clean data. I'm just lucky I hadn't put my real samples in, yet."

Jonathan shook his head in chastisement.

"Please take care with your work, Corrie. Reagents aren't free, you know. If you aren't confident, get Mara to shadow you on the mass spec."

"Yes, good idea," Corrie said automatically. "I'll be more careful, I promise."

"I'm looking forward to seeing your data tomorrow at lab meeting," he said. "If you do run the mass spec today with your real samples, pop them in a slide at the end, even if it's raw data."

"Will do," said Corrie.

Jonathan left, and Corrie scrambled to collect reagents. She needed to do a run on her bacterial samples. They were ready, but she hadn't run them through the mass spec yet because she had been too busy with her slime protein. She had to focus. With Jonathan so annoyingly observant lately, she had to be on her toes.

Her lab mate Mara came up a few minutes later. Bouncy red curls formed a halo around her head, and she plopped into a nearby chair.

"Hi Corrie. Jonathan said you need help on the mass spec?"

Corrie grumbled inside. She knew how to use the machine just fine. She didn't need someone else shadowing her every move. But Mara was only being nice, so Corrie didn't let her feelings show.

"I wouldn't mind trying it on my own, but can I ask you if I have any questions?"

"Sure thing," she said, and bounced away. Corrie sighed, grabbed a pipette, and got to work.

FLINT

Flint checked his fishing line again.

"This is the slowest, stupidest sport ever invented," he said. "Why anyone does this for fun is beyond me."

"You never sit still for long enough," said Gavin. He peered through binoculars. "That's your problem. Fishing is supposed to be relaxing, interspersed with bouts of action."

"Not nearly enough action," Flint grumbled. "What the hell are those idiots doing out here, anyway? They never put out fishing lines, they don't scuba dive, they don't travel enough distance for cruising. What is their game?"

Flint fell heavily onto a padded bench on the aft deck of their liveaboard powerboat. Say what you wanted about their employer, but Miles Callahan knew how to ride in style. Flint had taken the master cabin because Gavin had been slow to arrive when they were leaving, and he didn't feel bad about it in the slightest. It was luxurious with a capital L. Not that Gavin's cabin didn't have gold-plated drawer handles, too, but the king-size bed in the master cabin was a nice touch.

Gavin rested his elbows on the arms of his deck chair to steady his binoculars. Flint gazed past him in the same direction.

"They're not even doing anything," Flint said. "The scrawny one isn't on deck, and the blond one is just sitting there. This is seriously the most boring mission we've ever been assigned."

"You do like to complain, don't you?" said Gavin. "I think it's peaceful, drifting on the water, letting the waves rock the boat, occasionally watching two people from a distance. At least, it's peaceful when you're not belly-aching over there."

"I'm only saying, when this gig is up, I won't complain. I need more action than this. Why aren't we going in there and roughing them up like we did the Viking?"

"I told you," said Gavin with a thin veneer of patience. "Mr. Callahan wants stealth, at least until we know more. This Zeballos Artino knows something, but if we can tease it out of him first, that would be helpful. Don't worry, we only have to do this for a few days. Then we have clearance to approach them."

"Damn foolish name," said Flint. "Zeballos. Sounds like an idiot already. I'm looking forward to shaking the truth out of him."

"If these two keep doing nothing like they have been, you'll get your wish."

They sat in silence for a few minutes. There was little movement from the other boat, and none from the fishing line. Flint stood up.

"I'm going to check the instruments," he said. "At least I can watch fish swimming around on the depth sounder for some activity. Better than watching the paint dry out here."

Gavin nodded and continued to look through his binoculars. Flint plodded to the front. His work with Tangled Net was varied, he'd give it that. Although this gig was currently tedious, it had its moments. It beat a desk job, that was sure. And the perks didn't hurt. He ran his hand along a wooden railing, buffed to an almost mirror-like polish.

The driver's spot was as luxurious as the rest of the boat. Pristine white leather covered the seat. Flint hesitated, then carefully dusted off his backside before he sat. It would be just like him to stain that expanse of creamy white.

Miles Callahan had spared no expense when buying instrumentation for this boat. Flint didn't even know what half this stuff was. Lights flashed, speakers pinged, and screens showed numbers and images that he didn't understand. Gavin had been briefed on all that. Flint was happy to leave the technical stuff to Gavin. He knew his strengths, and all this tech jazz wasn't it.

He did know the depth sounder, though. This was a high-tech one, where he could practically see individual fish swimming under the boat. He watched them flounder around, making random patterns with their movements. There were a lot of fish down there today. Out of boredom, he started to count the ones on the screen.

A light flashed from a console beside the depth sounder. Flint thought that it was for hearing whales or something, but he couldn't remember. The light flashed again. He wondered if he should stick his thumb over it, so it didn't distract him from his count. Movement on the depth sounder screen drew his eye back.

Fully half of the fish under their boat were moving in the same direction, all together. Flint blinked and looked closer. When he convinced himself that it wasn't an illusion, he shouted to Gavin.

"Oy! Come up front, Gavin!"

A moment later, Gavin appeared, his smooth forehead creased in annoyance.

"There's no need to shout," he said stiffly. "You can fetch me if you wish to talk."

"Look at this." Flint pointed at the screen. "There's a bunch all moving together. It just started."

Gavin leaned closer to look. They watched the fish. More swam past from beyond their boat, all moving in the same direction.

"This just started?" said Gavin finally.

"Yeah, a minute ago. They were swimming around randomly before."

Gavin went to the deck and looked over the edge. Flint followed him. There was nothing but green water for a long moment. Flint was about to stand upright, when he saw it. A flash of silvery iridescence, a sleek fish body, and a... horn? Flint blinked in surprise.

Gavin leaned back with a whistle, then he moved swiftly inside. Flint trailed after him, still trying to figure out what he had seen. Gavin looked at the instrumentation.

"The fish are still moving on the depth sounder. I don't suppose you noticed anything else change at the same time?" His voice held no hope that Flint would understand the consoles, but Flint brightened.

"Yeah, I did. This light started blinking, for whales or whatever. It's been going non-stop ever since, maybe every ten seconds."

Gavin pressed some buttons and read the tiny screen next to the light.

"There's a pulse of sound being emitted, at a frequency a little below human hearing. It can't be natural, not at ten-second intervals." Gavin looked at the depth sounder screen again. "Where are they going?"

Flint looked in the direction of the fish exodus. The boat they were watching was in the direct path. He and Gavin looked at each other.

"Who are they, and what are they doing?" Flint said quietly. Gavin frowned in thought.

"The boat must have turned on a sound emitter," he said finally. "That attracts a certain type of fish. See how they're swimming straight to the boat, as if drawn there."

"I wonder what kind of fish?" Flint said, understanding flickering at the edge of his mind.

"I think we can take a shrewd guess," said Gavin. He stared out the window for a moment. "Mr. Callahan would appreciate that emitter, I imagine. Especially if it attracts the fish he seeks."

"I feel bonus time coming up," Flint said. Gavin gave him a rare smile.

"Indeed."

Flint looked out the window again. The two men were climbing up the ladder of their boat, the scrawny one in a wetsuit and the blond one in nothing but a red speedo. Flint shook his head at the man's folly. The scrawny man looked in distress, and there was a lot of finger pointing at the ocean below him.

"I think they saw something," said Flint.

Gavin looked at the gesticulating men on the other boat, then he tapped his finger on the console in thought. "The emitter must be under the water for the sound to travel so well." He looked at Flint. "Flint, suit up. It's time for action."

Flint straightened. Finally, he could stop staring at waves and do something. This was what he was made for, what he was good at. The men on the other boat wouldn't know what hit them.

ZEBALLOS

Zeb knelt in the galley and flipped the switch in the lower cupboard.

"Get out of here," Jules said. He stepped over Zeb with an exaggerated motion. "This galley isn't big enough for you to roll around on the floor in."

"I'm going for a swim. Be back soon." Zeb straightened and caught Jules' nervous expression before he smoothed it over into his usual grin.

"Yeah, whatever. Just get out of my galley."

Zeb swiped a carrot stick then yelped when a tea towel flicked his back with ferocious speed. He moved to the deck and slid his flippers out of their place behind the life ring. His clothes were off in a moment, and he sliced through the air in an elegant dive to cut into the water like butter.

Nothing swam below the surface except microscopic algae and an occasional jellyfish that blobbed past his face. Zeb waited, eyes closed, enjoying the sensation of cool currents drifting past his skin. Every ten seconds, the sonar device made a low, eerie sound almost at the edge of his hearing.

After a minute of bobbing below the hull of the *Clicker*, a current tickled Zeb's sensitive skin. The tickle grew, larger and larger, until the current buffeted Zeb in the water. He opened his eyes, both terrified and elated by what he knew was coming.

A creature, dark as a shadow, snaked toward him. The ligan's head was visible now, and Zeb quailed before it. The head was easily taller than his torso, with a long, pointed snout. The mouth extended far back, indicating a wide jaw, with gills fanning out behind. Eyes were striated yellow and green and fixed on Zeb.

Zeb froze. Even if he wanted to escape, and only a small part of him did, there was no time. Anywhere he moved, the ligan would change course in an instant and follow him. The only thing to do was to stay put and hope that his mother was right.

With a rush of current that bowled Zeb over in a somersault, the ligan rushed by him. Bog-green scales almost brushed his skin. The ligan doubled back with a smooth movement strange in so large a creature and moved in a curling spiral around Zeb.

Zeb stayed as still as the currents would allow him and watched the ligan closely. So far, it hadn't opened its mouth to display what he knew was an impressive collection of sharp teeth as long as his forearm. Instead, it watched him back.

Zeb wracked his brains for lessons from his mother. Clicker had been able to charm any sea creature she encountered, be it whale or eel or perch. Zeb had done his best to learn, but she had left him when he was eight. He had practiced since then, of course, and was proficient at calming many underwater creatures, but this ligan was a whole new kettle of fish.

Zeb made a moaning noise in his throat, then a series of clicks. He repeated this a few times, adding with it some twists of his own body in a poor imitation of the ligan's smooth movements. The ligan slowed its swimming and watched him with what Zeb hoped was curiosity and not hunger. He continued to speak to the ligan with his best calming sounds.

The ligan stopped and held its massive head in front of Zeb for a long moment. Zeb ceased his movements and noises and simply stared into the yellow and green eyes. If his attempt didn't work, Zeb had nothing else to try.

A deep moaning noise started, and Zeb's heart jolted until he realized it came from the ligan. The serpent was responding to his overtures. Zeb didn't hold back his huge smile. He slowly held out a hand, and the ligan pushed its nose into it with a familiar gesture.

Zeb twirled in mid-water with a silly grin plastered to his face. The ligan swam in a circle, clearly imitating him. Zeb wondered how far the ligan would go, and he did a somersault. The ligan copied him with a massive movement, although far more gracefully. Currents buffeted Zeb's body as he watched the ligan's smooth length rush past him. The huge head emerged from the murk once more and pushed between Zeb's waiting arms. Zeb clung to the body of the great sea serpent as it tore through the water as fast as it could go.

If Zeb could have shouted with joy, he would have. As it was, his throat hummed involuntarily with his pleasure. Under his stomach, the serpent hummed in reply.

They swam like this for a few minutes, until Zeb's lungs reminded him of the air they needed. With reluctance, he let go and swam upward. He gasped a deep breath at the surface then looked around for the *Clicker*. They had swum so far that it was out of sight, although Zeb's keen sense of direction told him where it was. With another breath, he sunk below the surface once more.

The ligan was waiting for him. Before it rushed him, Zeb made a series of clicks that he used to indicate "home" or "back" to other fish he encountered. He had no idea if it would work for the serpent, but when it swam between Zeb's arms once more and took off, it was in the direction of the *Clicker*. Zeb's heart pounded with excitement and elation, and he'd never felt his mother's presence more than in the company of the ligan. He knew, without her having ever told him, that she had swum with one of the giant serpents before.

Too soon, they were near the *Clicker*. Zeb frowned as they drew closer. It was hard to tell, traveling at speed on the back of the serpent, but there were odd currents under the boat. They didn't remind Zeb of fish. The ligan slowed, and the hull of the *Clicker* emerged from the gloom.

Two scuba divers hovered near the bow. One had a tool with which he was trying to pry off the sonar device. Both divers had underwater propeller scooters dangling on cords from their wrists.

Zeb's anger flared. Who were these intruders, and why were they messing with his boat? Some sense of Zeb's anger must have transmitted to the ligan, because it stiffened. Zeb hesitated, then made a humming noise. It said "intruder."

The ligan shot forward with deadly accuracy. The divers hardly had time to look up before they were bowled head over heels in the water. The tool shot outward and sunk to the seafloor. The ligan curled around out of sight of the divers and prepared for another attack. For the first time, it opened its mouth, and Zeb saw the legendary teeth, knife-sharp and too many to count.

"Wait," he clicked and swam off the ligan as fast as he could toward the divers. Although he still felt the rage that had propelled him to tell the ligan to attack, his rational brain said it wasn't wise to order a mauling on two divers under his boat. With powerful kicks of his flippered feet, he shot toward the bow.

The divers were collecting themselves, clearly shaken and unsure what had happened. Zeb didn't allow them to recover. He swam next to the closest one and stared him in the face. The diver's eyes were wide behind his mask. Zeb pointed at the diver, then the hull, and made a cutting motion. Communicating with humans wasn't as easy underwater, but the diver seemed to understand. He waved at his fellow diver, and the two of them turned on their propeller scooters and flew away into the murk.

Zeb's heart beat faster than it usually did underwater, and his lungs started to pinch with their need for oxygen, but he didn't want to climb aboard without saying goodbye to the ligan. He called out with a hum. The massive serpent glided out of the dimness and circled Zeb. He stroked its smooth scales, humming in gratitude. Then he swam to the surface.

Once on board, he grabbed a towel then dripped into the galley. He wanted to turn off the switch as soon as possible, to not keep the ligan near the boat for no reason. It felt wrong to entrap such a magnificent creature, especially if he didn't intend to stay with it underwater.

"So?" Jules said, leaning against the counter as Zeb felt around for the switch. "See anything?"

"I made a new friend." Zeb told him about the ligan, and Jules turned from pale to amazed.

"You're a regular fish whisperer," Jules said. "Too bad women don't like fish as much as they do horses. You'd be killing it."

Zeb waved his comment away. Typical Jules, finding the lighthearted side of everything. But Zeb had more to tell.

"We saw two divers under the boat," he said. "I chased them away, but they were trying to take the sonar device. Who the hell are they, and how do they know about the device? Are they the same people who are following us?"

"Must be," said Jules, looking concerned. "Maybe we should get moving."

"Let's go to shore," Zeb said. He hated to say it—being away from the water went against his very core right now, what with the creatures and his incessant need to swim—but being at the mercy of unknown thieves didn't appeal either. "Find a crowded marina, turn off the sonar. Why don't we go to Victoria? I looked up my dad's weird storage locker, and it's there. I want to have a look inside."

"Victoria it is," said Jules. "I need to stock up on groceries, anyway."

Zeb headed to the wheelhouse after a quick change in his cabin. Jules pulled anchor and they set off south, around the tip of Vancouver Island. After a few hours, there was no sign of the powerboat behind them. Zeb checked his phone. He finally had reception closer to civilization. He dialed his voicemail to hear Krista's days-old message.

"Zeb. Where the hell are you? Matt Nielsen just called me. He was beat up by two goons looking for information about the unicorn fish. The slime is more than a hallucinogen—it's also an enhancer. Gives you extra speed and strength underwater. They really want to know more. Matt told them about you. I'm afraid they'll be after you next. Call me, okay? And watch your back."

Zeb hung up the phone and stared at it. That must be who the divers were, and why strange boats had been following the *Clicker*. They wanted to know more about the strolias. How had they known about the sonar device?

Zeb shook his head. Good thing he and Jules were heading to Victoria. It would be best to get lost in a bigger port, to be less exposed to searchers. He texted his sister back.

Got your message. Thanks for the warning. We're fine. I'll call later.

Zeb put his phone on the counter and looked out at the waves. It was breezy, with scuttling clouds and a few frothy whitecaps. The winds were changing, and there would be weather soon. Some spray hit the window and his heart tightened with longing.

He told himself sternly to pull himself together. There was no time to stop for a swim. He could handle a few hours without getting wet, surely. It was ridiculous if he couldn't. They needed to get to Victoria, lose the goons, hide themselves. A swim was not in the cards right now, even if he could visit with the ligan and see a school of strolias. He shook his head firmly. Not even then.

Thinking about the creatures reminded him of Corrie. She lived in Victoria. Maybe they could meet up. He wanted to hear about her research and see if she had made any progress identifying the strolia or analyzing the slime or whatever it was she was doing. He pulled the phone toward him and dashed out a text.

Hi Corrie, it's Zeb. I'll be in Victoria tonight. Do you have time to meet for coffee tomorrow and give me an update on your research?

He pressed send then had misgivings. He had planned to tell her all about his discovery with the sonar, to hear her theories about why it worked, and to tell her about the new creatures he had seen. She would be over the moon with the discoveries, he knew. But something nagged at him, warned him not to tell her. She was waffling about whether to tell her professor or not. She really wanted to bring the creatures to the public eye and further her career.

That was the last thing Zeb wanted. He'd rather she never told anyone about the creatures. If no one ever knew but him, Corrie, Jules, and Krista, he would be happy, at least until he understood what they meant to him. Corrie could tell the university at any moment. It was a risk he didn't want to take. She already knew too much. Giving her more fodder to sink her teeth into would be stupid.

His phone pinged.

Yes!!! I have lots to tell you. Meet you at that coffee shop beside Fisherman's Wharf tomorrow at three? So excited!!!

Zeb smiled. She texted just like she spoke: with emphasis and plenty of exclamation marks. He tried to ignore the thought of Corrie's ecstatic face if he told her about the ligan— she would bounce for joy, he knew—and attempted to convince himself that this was the right call.

He found himself missing the week she was on the boat. This past week with only Jules had been fine—Jules was good company, and more than enough conversation for Zeb, usually—but Corrie had brought a liveliness that Zeb didn't often encounter. It was foreign and sometimes uncomfortable, but when it was gone, he found he missed it.

Ten o'clock tomorrow wasn't far off, though. He would probably get too much of Corrie after a few minutes of her talking at him. The thought made him smile again.

CORRIE

Corrie pedaled faster, narrowly sneaking through an amber light. She was a few minutes late to meet Zeb, and she didn't want him to give up waiting. At least the rest of the way was flat. She stood and pumped her legs as hard as she could, cursing their shortness. Old character houses and trendy restaurants flew past, and she slowed at a four-way stop. When she was sure no cars waited, she barreled through.

The coffee shop was only half-full, and she easily spotted Zeb's white-blond hair and plaid shirt on the edge of the patio. He looked uncomfortable sitting by himself. Another patron, a pretty, blond woman a few tables over, eyed him with interest. She looked predatory, with too-bright lips and a busty top that Corrie took an instant dislike to.

Corrie's flash of irritation at the woman subsided when it was clear Zeb was oblivious to her attention. His fingers pushed his coffee cup around in circles, and he stared over the heads of other patrons to look longingly at the ocean beyond. Hadn't he just got off the boat? Maybe he was in culture shock, among so many people after a week of being on the water. Corrie stifled a giggle.

She quickly locked her bike and bounded up the steps. Zeb looked relieved when he saw her. He stood, and she threw her arms around him in a swift hug, which he awkwardly returned.

"It's so good to see you!" Corrie noticed a second, full coffee cup. "Is this for me? Thanks. I'm sorry I'm late. I forgot how far it is down here, and I took my bike." She sat down and sipped the coffee. "Oh, good, still warm. I'm not that late, then."

"It's fine," Zeb said. He was light on words, as usual, but Corrie could tell he was happy to see her by the smile in his eyes. "I'm glad you could make it."

"Oh!" Corrie's eyes widened and she put her cup down.

"Did Krista get a hold of you about the goons? There are some people chasing you, apparently. They beat up Matt Nielsen, can you imagine? They must mean business if they attempted to take on that guy."

"We did," Zeb reminded her. She laughed.

"Yes, I guess we did. But we did mean business, didn't we? But still, are you okay?"

"We're fine," he said. "I got Krista's message, but not before—" He paused, looking for words. "They started following us. And the *Clicker*, it has this weird device that makes a noise. We just found it the other day. The goons thought, for some reason, that it attracted fish."

"Attracted fish?" Corrie was puzzled. "Why would they think that?"

Zeb shrugged.

"I'm not sure. They tried to take it, though. I managed to fight them off. Then we came to Victoria to lose them. There are a lot of marinas here."

"Fight them off?" Corrie was horrified. "Are you okay? How about Jules?"

"We're fine," he repeated. "No harm done."

"Thank goodness," Corrie said. Her mind turned to the other strange news Zeb had revealed. "What's this device? Is it a common fishing instrument? Did it work, as in, did fish come closer when it was on?"

Zeb shrugged, more uncomfortably this time.

"No, it's not a normal device. I don't know why it's there, or what it's really for. I don't know if it worked. We only had it on for a short time." He didn't meet Corrie's eyes when he said this.

Corrie's eyes narrowed. Was there something he wasn't telling her? Then again, why was she surprised? It seemed his style, and really, he didn't owe her anything. They barely knew each other. Even though their shared experiences made Corrie feel that they were close, he obviously didn't feel the same way.

That was fine. To each their own. One would think that their shared secret was enough of a bond to promote some trust, but apparently not.

"How is your analysis going?" Zeb said, clearly trying to change the subject. "Have you found anything interesting?"

Corrie was still annoyed at the secrecy, but she let him steer the conversation away.

"Yes, you won't believe it. The genome work came back, and the unicorn fish is definitely in the salmon genus, but it's not any species that has been recorded before. I would love to isolate the differences between the unicorn fish and its next closest salmon relative, but it would take more funding than I have to fully sequence each genome."

"How much?" Zeb asked. Corrie laughed.

"How much inheritance did you get? I don't even know, but it would be a lot. I can find out for you if you're keen. There's more, though. I've been looking at the proteins in the slime. The composition is interesting. There's a lot of similarity between the slime proteins and pufferfish toxins, although it clearly isn't as deadly. But the weird thing is a signal that keeps cropping up in every sample. I'm sure it's not an equipment malfunction, because the controls are clean. It could be contamination, but it's identical across every sample, so it seems unlikely. I don't know what it is, but I'll keep checking into it. I hesitate to say that it's a new amino acid, because that would be insane, but I don't know." She smiled ruefully at Zeb, who held onto her every word with intense interest. "This whole thing is insane already, isn't it? New species, strange effects. Who knows what we'll find?"

Zeb leaned back, looking like he was digesting her words.

"Why would a new amino acid be insane?" he asked. Corrie spread her hands.

"There are only twenty-two amino acids, and they are the building blocks of all proteins. They've all been described since the nineteen-thirties, I think. I don't know, it feels like finding a new element. It happens, but that I would be the one to do it…" Corrie trailed off, overwhelmed. "Forget a journal paper. We're talking Nobel prize, here." She shook her head to dismiss her fantasies. "But I need to do way more testing before we can say anything like that. And I'm doing this all in the evenings to avoid awkward questions. My supervisor is already sniffing around with suspicion. And I have to take it slow, since I'm essentially stealing supplies from the lab to do these analyses. It's either that, or let my supervisor in on the secret, and I'm not ready to do that, yet."

Zeb looked thoughtful.

"Since the unicorn fish and Sucker are connected, like you said—"

"Symbiotically," Corrie clarified.

"Symbiotically," Zeb said. "Would they be related at all? If you had a sample from Sucker or another different fish, would that help?"

"A sample from Sucker? That would be incredible. But I don't envy the person collecting it." Corrie looked at Zeb with consideration. "Could it be done without killing yourself?"

"Probably not," Zeb said. "It would be a suicide mission. If we ever saw one again, of course. But I just wondered if Sucker would have this other amino acid, since they're connected."

"That's assuming transfer between the species—possible, but I wouldn't assume it—or they somehow both evolved to have the same amino acid. That feels unlikely, given that they are presumably not under the same evolutionary pressure. I mean, one's a giant octopus." Corrie drummed her fingers against the table. Zeb stared at her, waiting to hear her next thought. "Or, they both ingest the same food source that contains this amino acid. Whatever it is."

Zeb frowned. A thought struck Corrie.

"What did you mean, another different fish? Have you seen something else?" Corrie leaned forward in her intensity. Zeb shook his head, a little too quickly for Corrie's suspicions.

"No. It's just—my mum's stories. There were lots of different fish, and they all seemed to be connected."

"You think there is some isolated stretch of ocean where mythical sea creatures hang out together?" Corrie paused, then the absurdity of her statement made her laugh out loud. "That would be awesome, wouldn't it? Our very own Atlantis."

Zeb smiled at her mirth, but it didn't reach his eyes.

"I'll keep you updated on any new findings," Corrie said. "I'm working hard, but science is slow. Especially when we get weird results, and I have to run things over and over to make sure that we're not seeing contamination. And that's when the analyses go well the first time, which is never."

"I understand. I'm interested in whatever you find, whenever."

"Hey," Corrie said. "How long are you in town?"

"Overnight, at least. Jules is picking up groceries."

"I'd like to see Jules again. Why don't you two come to my house tonight? We'll get pizza, you can meet my roommates, have some drinks. It'll be fun." As quiet as Zeb was, she found she had missed him. He didn't speak much, but she could tell he was always listening and interested in what she had to say. Besides, she had enough to say for both of them. It was refreshing. He was very calm, too. She felt more at ease than she had all week.

"Yes, that sounds great," Zeb said quickly, looking pleased. "We'll be there. I know Jules wouldn't miss it."

KRISTA

Krista was in a meeting in the board room when her phone vibrated in her pocket. She ignored it—luckily it was on such a low setting that no one else appeared to hear it—and continued listening to the meeting. She was only there to hear the partners talk about a recent ruling and to take notes, which grated her pride. She'd learned to swallow that the first week here, though, and now she could put on a carefully neutral face while doing menial jobs despite her disdain on the inside. One day, she'd be partner, too. That would be a great day.

She pretended to look attentive while she wondered who had called her. There weren't many who would. Her mother, maybe, but she usually called on Sundays, not when Krista was at work. Her few friends wouldn't call her—they'd text instead. So, it could only be…

Her back stiffened. Zeb. It had to be. His text hadn't completely reassured her, not with the goons still on his tail. If he was calling, that was a good sign, she hoped. Unless it was a hospital or Jules calling, instead. Her mind sent her down unpleasant paths, and she desperately wanted to pull out her phone and check.

"Ms. Artino?" one of the partners said. "Did you take down that last bit?"

"If you could repeat it once more, to make sure it's accurate," she responded with her hands at her keyboard. Zeb was fine. There was nothing she could do in the next half-hour to make a difference, anyway. She was a professional. She could concentrate on this meeting and ignore her little brother's phone call. She'd never make partner if she couldn't do that. Even if it was a potential distress call. She gritted her teeth and willed the partners to hurry up.

As soon as the partners shuffled their papers at the conclusion of the meeting, Krista slammed her laptop shut and strode from the board room. She ducked into the lunchroom and whipped her phone out of her pocket. Zeb answered on the second ring.

"Hey, Krista."

Krista let out a huge sigh of relief.

"You big idiot. You had to wait that long to call? I left that voicemail days ago. What if you'd been fed to the fishes by now?"

"I texted you when I got it," said Zeb, sounding defensive. "We were out of cell range."

"Yeah, whatever." Krista lowered her voice when a colleague came in to grab something from the fridge. Zeb took the opportunity to change the subject.

"We're in Victoria now. I left Jules to do the grocery shopping."

"It's a wonder the idiot is as skinny as he is, with the way he cooks. You know I gained three pounds last week on the boat?" She brought them back to the topic that Zeb was clearly trying to avoid. "Any sign of the goons that beat up Matt?"

"Don't freak out, but actually, yes," Zeb said calmly. Krista's stomach flopped over.

"What?" she whispered loudly into the phone. Her grip on the device was deathly tight. "What are you talking about?"

"A boat was tailing us for a while. Then they dived under the boat and were trying to steal some noise-emitting device that Dad installed on the hull. I chased them off, then we high-tailed it to Victoria to lose them. Pretty sure we did."

Krista tried to steady her breathing. It could have been worse. Zeb was in one piece, and the goons hadn't found out anything. A thought struck her, and she narrowed her eyes in suspicion.

"How did you chase them off?"

There was a pause.

"I, uh, swam under and kind of waved at them to go," Zeb said with diffidence. Krista raised an eyebrow. She knew he couldn't see her, but it wouldn't stay down at Zeb's explanation. Her incredulity probably crossed the phone lines, it was so strong.

"And they just went. Were you wearing a wetsuit and mask while you 'waved' at them?" She layered as much sarcasm as she could manage on the words, which was an impressive amount. She had a lot of practice.

"No." Zeb sounded defiant. "But they went away, and we left them behind, so that's done. Krista," he said, with a clear change of tone and topic. "Can you get me some more jellyfish from Chinatown? I'm almost out."

Krista allowed herself to be distracted. It was true, there wasn't much more they could do about the goons, except keep an eye out for them. She thought about what Zeb had said.

"What do you mean, you're almost out? I just bought a new bag for you last week. You can't have gone through it already."

"Yeah, well, I did. I bought some here in Victoria, but it's really expensive. Get me a couple of bags, will you?"

"Can eating that much be good for you?" Krista said. "I guess there's not much to them, but still."

"Nothing else does the trick," Zeb said. "Whoa, that was weird."

"What?" Krista was on high alert again. Zeb would give her gray hairs soon, the way he went about things. It was probably good she hadn't pumped out a few babies by now, the way some of her high school friends had. She couldn't handle the stress, if it were anything like keeping an eye on Zeb.

"I felt woozy. It's gone now."

"You sure?"

There was a pause, then a crashing noise.

"Zeb?" Krista yelled into her phone, heedless of anyone at work hearing her. "What's going on?"

She heard more crashing and shuffling, then Zeb's voice in the distance saying, "Sorry, sorry." There was a rustling, then he breathed heavily into the phone.

"Krista? Still there?"

"What the hell was that?"

"I fell. Knocked over a stand of postcards. Everything went gray for a moment, it was weird. I'd never felt that before." He paused, then continued in a more collected tone. "It's fine now, though."

"Are you sure? You've never come over faint before. You should get yourself checked out."

"I haven't been to the doctor since I was in elementary school. I feel fine—there's no need to break my streak now."

"Typical man," Krista grumbled. "If it happens again, you should."

"Yeah, yeah," Zeb said, but she knew he didn't mean it.

"And keep an eye out for those goons. They might find you again. They seem to have resources."

"I've already encountered them once and survived to tell the tale," Zeb said. "Stop worrying so much. And don't forget my jellyfish."

"You're infuriating," Krista said. "Talk to you later, weirdo."

"Bye, Krista."

After she hung up, a cold feeling settled in her gut. Zeb's cravings were one thing, but coupled with a fainting episode, that was worrisome. She was forcibly reminded of the beginning stages of his mother's illness, the one that eventually killed her, the one that doctors had never been able to diagnose. She had suffered from fainting spells, too.

Zeb obviously hadn't been reminded of it. He was only eight when she had died, though. Krista had been ten, and it had frightened her to see Clicker collapsing on the kitchen floor and needing to be helped to the couch. Krista had tried to distract Zeb whenever it had happened, until Clicker had recovered sufficiently.

Maybe she was reading too much into it. It was a warm day, or at least it appeared so through the windows of her air-conditioned office. Maybe he had too much sun. There was nothing to worry about. Probably.

JULES

Jules clutched two full bags of groceries in each hand. The automatic doors whooshed open and he stepped out into the heat of a glorious summer's day. The bags were heavy, and he wished he'd had the foresight to bring a backpack for the bus ride home. Oh, well, maybe it would build up his biceps a little. He could never compete with Zeb's physique, not having the fortitude nor the interest to swim for insane amounts of time, but a little more bulk wouldn't go amiss.

It was probably a lost cause, though. The sooner he accepted his skinny frame, the happier he'd probably be. His ex-girlfriend Carole hadn't minded it. Or, maybe she had, and that was one more unspoken reason she'd dumped him. It was possible.

Jules hefted the bags more firmly in his hands and strode to the bus stop with resolve. When he was halfway there, his arms burning, a ringtone sang from his pocket.

He shuffled all four bags to one hand before giving up and dropping them on the pavement. He fished the phone out of his pocket. The screen said that Krista was calling. He swallowed his surprise and answered.

"To what do I owe the dubious pleasure of a phone call from the great Krista Artino?"

"Hi, doofus," Krista's voice crackled through the earpiece. "Glad I caught you. I just talked to Zeb."

"Who probably enjoyed speaking to you more than I do."

"Yeah, yeah, I'll keep it short. Zeb isn't taking these goons seriously, the ones following you two. I need you to look out for him. Just another pair of observant eyes, you know."

A flash of annoyance heated Jules' chest. Krista must think he bounced around with his eyes closed. Jules was there with Zeb when Krista wasn't. He was the only one watching out for him right now. He pushed down the irritation and answered mildly.

"Yes, of course, I'll watch out for him."

"Good. He swam in front of the goons, you know."

"Yes, I know."

"Well, neither of you seemed to pick up on this, but the goons are looking for information about an underwater strength enhancer. They think Zeb knows something. And after his performance, I think they have their answer. They'll be doubling-down on finding you two."

Jules felt chilled, despite the warm sun beating down on him. It was true, he hadn't thought of that. He glanced around him involuntarily, but nobody suspicious was watching him.

"Yeah, okay. Noted."

There was silence on the line.

"Krista? Anything else?"

"No, no." Krista sounded hesitant, which was most unlike her. "That's all. Bye, Jules."

Jules hung up but didn't pick up his bags immediately. What was Krista not telling him? And how was he going to keep Zeb out of trouble?

Corrie and Zeb chatted for a while longer at the coffee shop—namely, she talked, and Zeb listened—then she pushed her empty mug to the side.

"I should get going. It's a long bike ride home, and I need to make myself presentable after. You know, because you two haven't seen me at my most tired and sweaty yet." She winked, and to her surprise, Zeb laughed.

"It doesn't matter. Sweaty or not, you look the same to me."

Corrie wasn't sure how to take his comment. Did that mean she always looked good to him, or that he was so oblivious that he hardly saw her? She took refuge in teasing.

"That's because ladies glow, not sweat. What are you off to do now?"

"I found an old storage locker key in my dad's things," Zeb said. The statement dampened his good spirits, and Corrie was sorry she'd brought it up. "It's probably full of old junk, but I need to go through it. He was more of a packrat than I realized, if he had a locker for his stuff. I don't know why it's down here, though. He lived in Campbell River."

"Strange. Did he pass by here while fishing or doing tours?"

"Sometimes. Not a lot. I don't get it." Zeb shrugged. "Just another thing I'll never know."

Corrie thought that was an odd comment, but she let it pass. No doubt there were many things he wanted to ask his father, and now he didn't have a chance to. The thought made her sad. She vowed to call her parents tomorrow to say hello.

They parted ways, and Corrie biked hard on the way home. Her conversation with Zeb drifted through her mind, and again she puzzled over whatever he was hiding. It was hard not to take it personally, although Corrie was pretty good at letting affronts slide off her back.

She remembered the goons and shivered at the thought of

them finding the *Clicker* so easily. What sort of resources did they have, that they could pinpoint one old fishing vessel in the ocean? And where had she heard the name Tangled Net before?

Corrie finally coasted into her driveway. Despite what she told Zeb, she was more sweaty than glowing and desperate for a shower. Adrianna sat on the front step, painting her toenails.

"Hi there, beautiful," Adrianna greeted her. "Ready for the ball, I see."

"Ugh." Corrie threw her bike down and collapsed on the grass. "I'm done."

"What do you think?" Adrianna wiggled her toes at Corrie, which were a brilliant blue. Corrie grinned.

"Gorgeous. What's the occasion?"

"Summer is coming? I don't know, I don't need a reason. Patrick is coming over after work, how about that?"

"As opposed to every other day?" Corrie laid her head on the grass. "Makes sense to me. Hey, do you want pizza tonight? The guys from the boat, Zeb and Jules, they're coming over at seven."

"Sounds good. Patrick never says no to pizza."

Corrie gazed at the sky, where clouds were scuttling by in a stiff breeze. Adrianna tilted her head in Corrie's direction.

"What's up? You're never this quiet."

"I'm trying to remember where I've heard the name Tangled Net before. It won't come to me."

"You must have overheard Patrick," Adrianna said. "Tangled Net is a subsidiary of Miles Callahan's company. It's usually security and muscle, officially called Callahan Security. They call it Tangled Net internally." Adrianna closed the bottle of nail polish and admired her toes. "Don't ask me why. Maybe because no one is quite sure what they do, or maybe because their purpose is tangled when everyone uses them sometimes? Who knows?"

"So Tangled Net is run by Miles," Corrie said. Her stomach

twisted.

"Yeah, they report to him directly, as far as I know." She stood and waved to a car that was pulling into the driveway. "There's Patrick. We'll pick up something at the liquor store while we're out. See you at seven."

Adrianna hopped into the passenger's seat, and the car backed out of the driveway. Corrie sat, dumbfounded, at the news. Miles Callahan, the handsome, smooth-talking collector of exotic fish, commanded beatdowns of local fisherman for news of unicorn fish. She felt sick that she'd ever enjoyed his company. She'd been swayed by charisma and an interest in her world, and she hadn't wanted to look more closely. How could she have been so blind?

ZEBALLOS

Zeb stepped off the bus in front of a storage locker facility. On the wall of the facility, there was a mural of a giant mole digging a burrow filled with junk, and Zeb tightened his lips in distaste. That was what he was afraid of, that the locker would be full of literal trash that he would have to sort through. Maybe if it were too much to look at, he would conveniently lose the key and stop paying the bills. Eventually, they would shift the contents to the curb.

But maybe there was something of his mother's here. He owed it to himself to check. After all, what was one more storage locker to sift through? He had a whole apartment's worth of boxes to sort when he got home again. He almost groaned aloud at the thought, then he squared his shoulders and marched toward the building. Better get this over and done with. Dreading the task wouldn't make it go away any quicker.

It was a low-budget facility, typical of his father. There was no security except the keys for each locker and a blinking security camera that Zeb guessed wasn't monitored very closely. There was one problem, though—he didn't know the number of the locker.

Stymied, Zeb looked at the key on its ring. How could he figure it out, other than trying the key in each lock? Low security or not, he was pretty sure that tactic would raise alarm bells eventually.

The whale on the keychain leered at him with its too-wide smile. He snorted and flipped it over. Scratched into the metal on its back was the number forty-five.

"Glad you never owned a computer, Dad," Zeb muttered. "Your password would be 'password,' for sure."

Zeb strode to locker number forty-five, in the middle of a long row of identical doors. Paint peeled off the doorframe, but the lock seemed new enough. Zeb pushed the key into the lock and turned it with a resounding click. The door swung outward.

Inside was blackness, but when Zeb fumbled for a switch on the wall, the space glowed with dim light from a single bulb on the ceiling. After moving the endless boxes into his apartment, Zeb had expected the locker to be filled to the rafters, but it was nearly empty. Only five plastic bins lined the walls of the small space. Zeb blinked in surprise for a moment then shrugged and moved toward the closest box. It was time to see what George Artino felt he couldn't store in his own house, or even in his own town. Despite his certainty that the bins held nothing but junk, Zeb was intrigued.

The first bin contained a piece of equipment whose purpose Zeb couldn't begin to guess. Numerous tubes and wires protruded from a gray box made of plastic. It looked homemade. There were no instructions and no hint on what it was, so Zeb moved to the next box.

These contents were familiar. A finely woven fishing net cushioned a clear plastic bag holding a few pieces of dried jellyfish. The wrinkled white shapes were unmistakable to Zeb. A kitchen-grade food dehydrator filled the rest of the box.

Zeb lifted the bag with curiosity. Had his father netted and dried his own jellyfish for his mother? The snack was difficult enough for Zeb to find, and he couldn't imagine his hometown had been any more cosmopolitan when he was a child. Maybe he should take the net with him. It would be reassuring to not be dependent on Krista remembering to visit Chinatown, especially since his need had increased so dramatically.

Zeb peeked in the next two boxes, but both held bewildering contents. One box held an assortment of jars. Some looked like lotions, and some contained powders. One held liquid—Zeb could hear it sloshing around—but the glass was covered with duct tape and the jar's contents remained a mystery. The other box had a variety of small items, chief among them a bag filled with plastic contraptions with electronics glued on by someone without much knowledge or finesse.

Everything clearly had a purpose, even if Zeb couldn't fathom what it was. Why were these items so important to his father that they demanded a secret storage locker? Was this from his life before Zeb?

A wave of frustration and resentment washed over him. This was just another secret. The man had been full of them. Zeb was less surprised by the revelation of the storage locker, and more surprised that he himself had expected something straightforward from his father.

When he opened the last box, he was relieved to see three notebooks. Finally, he could get some answers, or at least understand what the items in these boxes were. He opened the topmost notebook, expectant and hopeful. His heart fell when he recognized the boxy lines of the Greek alphabet.

"Really, Dad?" he murmured. "You couldn't make anything easy, could you?"

Zeb could speak Greek decently, thanks to a summer his paternal grandmother had spent with them when he was ten. She only spoke Greek, but Zeb was excellent at languages and conversed fluently with her after a few weeks. Reading Greek, however, remained a mystery. He would have to familiarize himself with the alphabet before painstakingly deciphering the language. He sighed.

"Another useless inheritance. Thanks, Dad." He tucked the three notebooks in his backpack. He considered leaving the devices behind—they weren't any good to him, especially since he didn't know what they did—but he paused at the thought that the notebooks were the key to understanding. Corrie might be interested in the contents of the jars. He bundled everything into one bin and heaved it in his arms, before he locked the storage door behind him and left the key in the lock. The storage facility could reclaim their space, now. He was done with it.

CORRIE

Corrie sat on the grass, stunned, for a few minutes. She didn't know what to think. Miles Callahan was in charge of Tangled Net. He had told the goons to beat up Matt Nielsen for information. He had given the order to follow the *Clicker* and had tried to steal the sonar device. Corrie supposed she should count her blessings that Zeb and Jules hadn't been pummeled by the goons' fists.

She swallowed, feeling sickened by the whole thing. Who would do that? Who would think that violence was the answer for extracting information? Had he even tried sitting down with Matt and simply asking? Miles was certainly charming enough for that tactic to work, most of the time.

At the thought of Miles' charm, Corrie's sick feeling intensified. To think she had thought he was a nice guy. If she were completely honest with herself, she might have even had a little crush on him. She shuddered at the thought now.

She had an impulse to call Adrianna, get Miles' phone number, and hash it out right there and now. Only the gut feeling that this was much bigger than a phone call could solve stopped her. She dithered, wondering what to do. She should tell Zeb, certainly, but he was coming over in a few hours. That sort of news would be better in person.

Krista would want to know. Maybe she would have a better idea than Corrie about what to do next, where to take this information. Not that hot-headed Krista was the ideal confidante, but Corrie needed to talk to someone who cared as much as she did, and who could help her brainstorm a plan. Miles spent most of his time in Vancouver, she knew, and that was where Krista lived. Who knows, proximity might help. She pulled out her phone.

"Hello?" Krista's voice sounded surprised and suspicious when she answered the ring. Voices babbled in the background. Corrie cleared her throat.

"Krista, it's Corrie. I figured out Tangled Net."

There was a rustle, then the background noise receded.

"I'm listening."

"It's a company called Callahan Security, known as Tangled Net to insiders. It's owned by—"

"Miles Callahan," Krista breathed. "Damn it."

"You know him?"

"Know of him. This is bigger than I thought. What the hell is Miles Callahan doing embroiled in all of this?"

"He invests in futurist tech and products, doesn't he?" Corrie said. "He's after the unicorn fish slime, especially if he knows it's an enhancer, like Matt said."

"Yes, he wants to turn around and sell it to the highest bidder." Krista clicked her tongue repeatedly. "Listen, I might know someone who knows something."

"I don't know whether that sounds promising or not," Corrie said. It wasn't like Krista to be so vague. Krista sighed.

"I've heard rumors that he's being investigated. For what, I don't know, but I might be able to find out something that could help. Damn it!" Krista exploded. "I should go down to Callahan offices and confront him myself."

"And be taken away by Tangled Net?" said Corrie. "No, don't. That sounds promising, about the investigation. Maybe he'll be too busy defending himself to bother with Zeb. Let him think we don't know, yet. I don't want to force a move. Miles has lots of resources, so let's tread carefully. I don't think the goons have traced the *Clicker* to Victoria yet. Zeb and Jules will be at my house this evening. I don't know what their plans are after that, but I could suggest they keep moving."

"Yes, do that." Krista swore again. "I hate the big guys getting away with crap because they have 'resources.' That's why I went into environmental law, you know."

"I didn't know that, actually." Corrie's respect for Krista

increased. "I wonder what Miles is being investigated for."

"Not sure yet. Probably environmental infractions. I'll try to find out. Let's take this bastard down."

ZEBALLOS

Zeb was in his cabin with a towel around his midriff. They were due at Corrie's in an hour, and he was deciding what to wear. He'd hastily grabbed a few clothes during their brief sojourn onshore up island, fully expecting to see only Jules for most of their time away. He hadn't anticipated a gathering at Corrie's house and meeting her roommates.

He lay out a few shirts and pants on his bunk and gazed at them in growing despair. They were work clothes, plain and simple. He wondered if it were too late to go out and buy something, then chastised himself for being such a girl about it. One of the outfits would do. He just had to pick one.

He looked at them for a moment longer, then decided he'd choose later. He turned to the tiny mirror above his chest of drawers. His hair was short, so there wasn't much he could do with it, but he pushed it one way and then another to see what it looked like.

Jules pushed the door open and caught sight of Zeb messing with his hair. He gave a broad grin through a mouthful of toothbrush and foamy toothpaste.

"Who are you trying to impress?"

"No one," Zeb said automatically. It was true. He didn't need to impress anyone. Corrie had already seen him at all hours, in all states, while on the boat the other week. The roommates were unknown entities, but he didn't need to worry about them. Chances are he'd never see them again after tonight. He roughly brushed his hair into its normal place.

"Oh, really," said Jules with an air of supreme disbelief.

"I'm cleaning up after being on the boat for so long. I'd forgotten what my hair feels like without salt in it."

"Sure, sure," Jules said. "Do you know something about these roommates that I don't?" Jules peered into Zeb's mirror, prodded his shaggy hair, then shrugged. "That's the best I've got. It'll have to do." He glanced at Zeb's bunk and the clothes laid out on it. He pointed at a plaid shirt and the more worn set of jeans. "Don't wear that, whatever you do. Krista would mock you forever."

Jules left with a snicker. Zeb rubbed his face and sighed, wishing tonight was already over and done with. He could face a giant sea serpent easily enough, but a party was daunting.

Zeb and Jules arrived at Corrie's doorstep a few minutes after seven, thanks mainly to Zeb's chivvying of Jules. Corrie lived in a suburban neighborhood close to the university, full of seventies-era houses populated by student rentals and young families. Corrie's next-door neighbor had three tiny bicycles parked on the front stoop.

Jules rang the doorbell before Zeb had a chance to collect himself. There was a thumping from inside, as if someone was running downstairs, then the door was flung open.

Corrie beamed at them. She wore a sparkly top that revealed plenty of cleavage and tight dark jeans.

"Jules! Zeb! So nice to see you." She flung her arms around Jules, who laughed, then she hugged Zeb briefly. Zeb caught the scent of something floral, maybe jasmine, before she pulled away. He had a fleeting moment of wishing it wasn't such a speedy embrace. "So glad you could make it. Come in, come in."

"We brought libations." Jules held out a bag from the liquor store. "Beer for us slobs, and wine for you so we could pretend to be classy guests."

Corrie giggled.

"We drink everything here, you'll be fine. Come on up and meet everyone." She paused, then said, "I need to tell you something about the goons. We'll talk later, okay?"

Zeb nodded, curious but willing to follow Corrie's lead. She bounded up the stairs. Jules joined her, clearly buoyed by the thought of drinks and people to talk to. Zeb followed more slowly, steeling himself to appear sociable. It wasn't that he didn't like people. It was just that he had a hard time thinking of things to say, and everyone seemed to be more comfortable in groups than he did.

Corrie's comments on the boat, about him never laughing, hadn't left him. It didn't matter what she thought of him, not really. Still, he didn't want to be known as the boring guy. He could try to be engaging. It wasn't impossible, although it had been a while since he'd cared enough to try. They'd had a fun party on the boat after they defeated Matt and Sucker, hadn't they? He could do that again. Zeb took a deep breath and climbed the last of the stairs.

Everyone was in the kitchen. Despite it being crowded, there was a cozy feel to it. Corrie waved her hand around the room.

"Everyone, this is Zeb and Jules."

A chorus of hellos greeted the two. Corrie pointed at each person in turn.

"This is my roommate Adrianna and her boyfriend Patrick." A pretty woman with strawberry-blond hair waved at them next to a dark-haired man wearing a tee shirt. "My roommate Sophie, but we all call her Trip." A serious-looking woman with a mischievous twinkle in her eye looked them up and down and gave a nod with her mouth slightly upturned. "And my boyfriend, David."

Zeb looked at the last man. His blond hair was carefully styled, and he looked sharp and put-together in a shirt and slacks, the buttons on his shirt opened near the neck just enough to appear casual. He slipped an arm around Corrie's waist when she introduced him. Zeb felt a flare of satisfaction at Corrie's clear discomfort at the awkwardly familiar gesture, then squashed it. David, however, looked smug, and Zeb took an instant dislike to him.

"Hello, Jules." David grabbed Jules' hand, who shook David's with bemusement. "Zeb." David's handshake was firm to the point of discomfort, and Zeb found himself gripping David's hand tightly to preserve his own fingers. "Nice to meet you. Corrie was so excited to win that award. You did a really great thing offering that."

Zeb nodded, attempting nonchalance.

"Yeah, I wanted to support science, you know. It seemed like a good way to do it."

He gave a half-glance at Corrie, who nodded slightly with wide eyes. It seemed she hadn't told David about the strolias and brigar, which pleased Zeb. She took her secrecy seriously, if she hadn't even told her boyfriend. He wondered how long they'd been dating. A stuffy guy like David didn't fit with Corrie's bubbly good nature, in his opinion.

He remembered his vow to seem engaging. He tried a smile.

"The sampling went well, though, didn't it, Corrie? You got some good data?"

"Oh, yes, it was so great. Obviously, early days yet, so much analysis to do in the lab, but we did so many stations! And…" Corrie ran away with her thoughts, and Zeb breathed easy for a minute. He could do this. It was pretty easy with Corrie. She carried the conversation, which was helpful. He planned out what topic he might bring up next, so he wasn't unprepared during the next lull in conversation. Not that Corrie would ever let a lull happen. He nearly smiled at the unlikely notion of silence with her around.

Jules had struck up a conversation with the other roommates, in his easy way he had. Adrianna laughed at something he said, Patrick grinned, and Trip looked at him with an appraising eye. Zeb felt a moment of jealousy for his friend, but it was quickly washed away by gratitude. Jules would bail him out if he got stuck, conversation-wise. He was a good wingman. Or was Zeb the wingman? Zeb was probably the wingman at parties— Jules was the star, and he played the supporting role. Zeb dragged himself out of his irrelevant thoughts and back to Corrie's words.

"…And once I run those samples, I'll know much more," Corrie finished. David looked at Zeb.

"What do you do, Zeb, when you're not hosting early-career scientists?"

Corrie looked at him with raised eyebrows. Zeb hesitated but then spoke with assurance.

"I'm between jobs right now. Enjoying the inheritance. I felt that a little self-exploration was wise before I jump into my next career move."

The words came easily. He had fallen back to the "rich kid" persona, which Corrie still believed. He didn't like lying to her, not after what they'd been through together, but David was another story. He looked like the kind of man who valued career and job over everything, and Zeb didn't need to be made to feel inferior because he was considering roofing in the autumn. He got the sense that David wouldn't respect that.

David nodded.

"Not a bad idea. Better to be confident in where you're going, instead of following the wrong path for too long." David smiled down at the petite Corrie and squeezed her waist. "I've been lucky to have known my career path from an early age. I'm an accountant, just got headhunted for a big firm. It's looking good."

"Congrats," Zeb said politely, but he was spared any further talk of accountancy by the doorbell ringing. Corrie wriggled out of David's grasp.

"Oh, good, the pizza's here," she said. "I'll get the drinks. Zeb, what'll you have?"

"Beer, please," he said gratefully. Maybe talking to David wouldn't be such a trial with some alcohol to soften the edges. Trip moved toward the doorway, and Jules followed.

"I'll help," he said. Trip slipped her arm through his and pulled him down the stairs. Adrianna beckoned Zeb over.

"So, you're the famous Zeballos," she said with a laugh. "We've heard so much about you."

Zeb's cheeks warmed, but he managed a small grin.

"Good things, I hope."

"Oh, of course. The magnanimous captain, dispensing science opportunities for the truly fortunate." Adrianna smiled to show she was teasing. "Seriously, that's pretty great you did that. And I hear you might be going out again?"

"I have some more time, and Corrie had more samples to get," Zeb said. "It works for both of us."

"Amazing. I wish I had a benefactor, who would get me started on my own vet clinic." Adrianna gazed into the distance for effect. "Rhodes to Recovery Animal Hospital, Specializing in Exotics. Can't you see it now?"

"It's a good dream," Zeb said. "Don't forget it. Sorry I can't be more help. I have some money from the inheritance, but not an endless pot."

"Oh!" Adrianna put her hand on his arm to support her laughter. "I wasn't fishing, honest. I have another year before I graduate, anyway. No worries."

Zeb smiled, but their conversation was interrupted by the arrival of pizza. The food served as common ground, and Zeb managed to have a few lighthearted exchanges about the different types of pizza that were ordered. The beer helped, too. He caught Corrie looking at him once or twice, but he couldn't understand her expression. Zeb still wasn't fully comfortable, but he was trying to appear sociable. He hoped he was succeeding.

JULES

Jules was in his element. There was beer, there was pizza—he could have cooked one better, obviously, but delivery was its own special breed and allowance had to be made for it—and there were plenty of lively people to talk to. He hadn't realized how starved for interaction he'd been on the boat. Zeb was great, he was Jules' best friend, but he wasn't a talker by any stretch. Jules was surprised his tongue hadn't shriveled in his mouth from lack of use.

Corrie was her usual lively self, laughing and making sure everyone had enough pizza. Her boyfriend David seemed fine—Jules hadn't really talked to him—and even Zeb was trying to be animated. Jules was proud of him. Adrianna was an easy conversant, and her boyfriend Patrick pitched in with witty quips frequently.

Trip, though, was something else. By Jules' third beer, the two of them had left the general conversation alone. By the time Trip had brandished a bottle of tequila and two glasses at him with a wicked grin, they were thick as thieves.

She was forthright, no doubt about it. But her words were softened by a clear interest in him as a person. It was if Krista had thought he was worth something instead of only existing to muddy her shoes.

"What do you do when you're not eating pizza at strange women's houses?" Trip tilted her head at him and sipped her glass. Jules shrugged easily, although he wasn't fond of the question. He liked his lifestyle, but people usually didn't have much to say after his answer.

"Odd jobs, mostly. Whatever needs doing. Right now, Zeb has me working deckhand and cook on his boat."

"Yes, Corrie mentioned your fabulous cooking. She couldn't stop talking about it."

Jules tried to look modest.

"People don't complain."

"Give yourself some credit. I burn water half the time." Trip rested her chin on one hand and looked at him seriously. "If you were on death row and had one last meal, what would it be?"

Jules smothered his grin and pretended to treat the question with as much seriousness as Trip was showing.

"Spaghetti carbonara. It's simple, but if done right, sublime. Am I allowed to cook it myself to make sure it's done properly?"

Trip smiled, and Jules melted a little.

"I'd choose *moules marinières*," she said. "Mussels in a white wine broth. I had it once on holiday. So amazing. Do you think the prison would take me to Paris for my last meal?"

"I'll visit you in prison and cook it for you," Jules promised. Trip reached out and stroked his cheek briefly.

"Maybe you could cook it for me sometime without me committing a felony."

"That's a little more ethical, I guess," Jules breathed.

Trip looked him up and down.

"Do you ever eat what you cook?" She reached out and poked him in the stomach. "You could do with putting on some meat."

Trip was too pretty for Jules to take much offense, although the comment smarted a little.

"I eat everything. Just one of those metabolisms, I guess."

"It's just not fair. Why is it always the men who can eat everything?" Trip leaned forward. "Next time I see you, I'm going to buy you a cheesecake. And watch you eat the whole thing."

They'd both had enough to drink that the comment felt suggestive.

"Drizzled with chocolate ganache," he said.

"Mmm, speak French to me. And don't forget a mountain of whipped cream."

Jules wanted to keep talking on this track, but he was afraid of embarrassing himself. He cleared his throat. "So, what do you do when you're not drinking tequila with strange men?"

"I'm a grad student like Corrie, but in electrical engineering."

Jules put his hands up in defense. Pretty and crazy smart? Trip was out of his league. He'd better make that clear. It was better that she drop him like a hot potato right now, rather than when he'd really fallen for her.

"Whoa, sounds way too complicated for me."

"Don't be silly," Trip said at once. "It's all about making connections. Take one wire." She slid her hand into Jules' palm. "And connect it in a circle." She took Jules' other hand and tucked the fingers into his. Her hand was warm. "That's when things really light up. I deal with that, but on a big scale. And I have to do math to figure it out. But that's the essence."

Jules melted a little more. She hadn't recoiled from his stupidity. Instead, she'd found a way for him to understand her world. He knew what she did was way more complicated that what she'd said, but it was the principle of the thing. She was willing to explain.

Trip's eyes twinkled, then she released his hand and held up the tequila bottle between them, somehow empty.

"This won't do," she said with a giggle. "I'll get us some more."

CORRIE

Corrie usually loved parties. Talking, laughing, eating, drinking—in moderation—it all made an evening complete. But this evening was draining her energy, and she knew why.

The tension from David radiated over her and had done so all evening. Corrie didn't understand what his problem was. No, that wasn't right. She guessed but tried to ignore the truth: David was jealous of Zeb. In whatever messed-up fantasy David had brewed in his head, Zeb was a threat.

Corrie didn't know where he had received that impression. She'd been no more than cordial to Zeb all evening, as befitted her benefactor and someone with whom she'd spent a week on a small boat. She had even been more touchy-feely than usual with David to alleviate his tension, to show him that she was his, but that hadn't dispelled the cloud. She was starting to get annoyed.

Corrie wondered if anyone else could sense David's mood, but she guessed not. He conversed easily enough, although words with Zeb tended to be more intense than with others.

Zeb, for his part, chatted with the rest well enough, which surprised Corrie. He usually wasn't so animated. He spoke with Adrianna while Corrie poured her and David more drinks. She was tempted to put aside her three-drink rule for tonight, if only to make David's mood palatable, but she resisted. She noted that Patrick was quietly eating pizza while Adrianna chatted to Zeb, and Corrie looked sourly at David when he wasn't looking.

"You're in vet school, you said," said Zeb to Adrianna.

"That's right."

"What's your favorite animal?"

Adrianna put her hand on her chin in a show of thought.

"Anything weird and wonderful," she said at last. "I want to specialize in exotics in my final year. The most usual ones are lizards and chinchillas these days. Everyone else has cats and dogs covered, and I'm not interested in sticking my hand up cow butts like a farm vet."

Zeb chuckled, an unusual sound from him. Corrie smiled to hear it.

"Fair enough. It doesn't sound appealing."

"I know, but don't tell anyone at the university. A fastidious vet would be laughed out." Adrianna winked at him. Zeb tilted his head in thought.

"How do you tell what's wrong with exotic animals? I guess there's a lot known about dog behavior, but what does an iguana do to tell you when it's sick?"

"Good question," Adrianna said. "There are some tells— lethargy, fewer droppings, lack of eating—but if you watch closely enough, everything speaks in its own way."

"I'll be back in a minute," David whispered in her ear. "Bathroom."

Corrie waved that she'd heard, and David departed. She didn't need the notification, but since David had been stuck to her side like glue all night, she guessed he'd felt compelled. She tuned into the others' conversation again while she sipped her drink.

"I've noticed that when diving," Zeb was saying, his face lively. This was clearly a topic that fascinated him. "If you watch closely enough, you can figure out what the fish want, what they're going to do next, what they think about you."

"That you're a big, bubble-blowing seal, I imagine," Adrianna said. Zeb smiled.

"Probably."

"No, it's true. Not enough people value the power of observation, in my opinion. And the value of talking to the animals. Even if they don't know what you're saying, volume and tone say so much. Also, body language. If you tower over an animal, of course it will be scared. Get down with them, and suddenly you can start the conversation."

Zeb nodded vigorously. Corrie wondered again at his interest. Maybe he was thinking of the unicorn fish and those stories of his mother's. But what was all this about communicating with them? As far as Corrie knew, Zeb had only ever seen the one unicorn fish in the tank. A vision of Zeb, soaking wet after "distracting" the giant octopus Sucker, flashed through Corrie's mind. What had really happened that day?

"I'm back," David said to her. She attempted a smile.

"Hey you. More pizza?"

"I think I'm full."

Adrianna moved to fill up her drink. David turned to Zeb, and Corrie took a deep breath to begin the buffering process again. She felt sorry for Zeb, who was here on her invitation and hadn't expected the Spanish Inquisition when he had arrived at her door. It looked like he was trying to make a good impression—he had even ditched his plaid for a black shirt that set off his hair—and Corrie wanted his evening to go well.

"So, Zeb," said David. "You said you were doing some self-exploration, in between career moves. Any thoughts on what next?"

"That's the joy of exploring," Zeb replied evenly. "I'm trying to figure it out."

"Yes, but any leanings? What are you good at, for example? That can help lead you in the right direction." David had a paternal air, which Corrie would have found amusing in any other situation. Zeb was the same age as David. "Do you like working with your hands, or outside? Do you work best on your own or with people?"

Zeb hesitated.

"Outside, I guess. And on my own, mostly. I'll figure it out eventually." He turned to Corrie. "Have you figured out where you want to sample next week?"

It was a transparent attempt to change the subject. Corrie latched onto it gratefully.

"Yes, I'll do the same as last time—water collection and diving for anemone samples—but I have some new ideas on locations. There are some high current regions that would be good to sample, and if we can manage it, I'd like to get to some of the northern inlets and the Queen Charlotte Sound. The sound has more upwelling, bringing more nutrients for growth, and the waters there are colder and more saline. The inlets are just the opposite. Basically, I want to find lots of different conditions so I can say more about how the bacteria react."

"Great," Zeb said.

"David," Adrianna said. She put her hand on his arm. "I've been meaning to ask you for some accounting advice. The clinic I work for, they need to hire a new bookkeeper, and I've been saddled with the task of hunting one down. What should I look for in a good bookkeeper?"

David let himself be led away. Corrie breathed a sigh of relief and was amused to hear Zeb do the same thing.

"Sorry about that," she said in an undertone. "I don't know what's up with him tonight."

"It's fine."

"This gives me a chance to tell you about the goons." Corrie looked around, but David spoke with animation about bookkeeping practices to Adrianna and Patrick, and Jules and Trip were tucked in a corner of the couch with a bottle of tequila between them. "I found out who gives the orders, who owns Tangled Net. It's Miles Callahan."

"Who?" Zeb looked confused.

"The owner of *Tomorrow*, that tech magazine. Miles is rolling in money, has his own private island and everything. He likes to invest in hot new opportunities, so the rumors go. Apparently, he'll do whatever it takes to get in at the right time."

She swallowed, feeling the shock once more of Miles' deception. Her disgust must have shown on her face, for Zeb looked concerned.

"Is there more?"

"I've met him. Patrick works for him, you see. I thought he was a nice guy, so it was a surprise to find out that he hired the goons to beat up Matt Nielsen. And come after you."

"I guess appearances can be deceiving," Zeb said, but he looked uneasy.

"I don't know what we can do with that information right now, but watch your back, okay?" Corrie touched his arm but withdrew it quickly before David could see. She knew he would get the wrong impression. "Miles has a surplus of money and a deficit of morals."

"That's not a good combo."

Corrie sighed.

"No, it's not. I called your sister and told her. She might be able to help, she's not sure. Miles is into shady stuff. She wants to take him down—"

"Of course," Zeb muttered.

"So, we'll see what she comes up with."

They were silent for a moment, digesting the notion of Miles and his goons. At least, that was what Corrie was doing. Who knew what Zeb thought about?

"I was thinking about your sonar device," Corrie said. "If the goons thought it attracted fish, they must have had a reason. Maybe it emits a frequency that carries well in the water. Whales can be heard kilometers away because of the frequencies they use. It's not uncommon. Even elephants make a low vibration that travels through the savannah so that other elephants can feel the call through their feet. It's a fascinating way to communicate. It's not inconceivable that this sonar device makes a sound that is attractive to a certain type of fish." She paused for a breath and thought about the implications of what she was saying. "No wonder the goons were after it. If it's not a usual fishing thing, then it must be new, and it might revolutionize fishing. That's exactly the kind of thing Miles would want to know about. Where did this device come from,

I wonder?"

Zeb looked overwhelmed at everything she had said.

"I don't know where it came from. Dad didn't tell me much." He frowned in thought. "I wonder what kind of fish might be attracted to this noise. It's right on the edge of human hearing. I can hear it, but Jules can't."

"Fascinating. I'd love to measure the frequency. Then we could start researching it more. Maybe next week, when I'm back on the boat."

From across the room, Jules and Trip burst into laughter. Jules pointed at Zeb.

"That wouldn't work on Zeb. That guy can hold his breath forever. Like, ridiculously long."

Jules was clearly drunk, and he and Trip subsided into chortles after his pronouncement. Corrie turned to Zeb and was surprised to see him looking pale and worried. He caught her eye and smoothed his expression.

"What was that about?" Corrie asked, intrigued. Zeb took a moment to answer.

"I free dive," he said finally. "It's a hobby of mine."

"Awesome," she said. "That explains the thin wetsuit, a bit. You need mobility normally for swimming. Although it's still freezing down there. Do you really work up a sweat? How do you manage when we're scuba diving and not moving much?"

"I don't get cold easily," he said, looking flustered.

"Do you go pearl hunting, or dive deep competitively? Have you seen anything cool down there? How did you get into it?"

"It's just for fun. My mum got me into it." He shrugged with a jerk. "There's always lots of interesting things under the water, but you know that—you scuba dive."

"Why free dive, though? You can go under for so much longer with a tank, and so much deeper."

Zeb looked at his drink, which was clutched tightly in one hand.

"It's so much freer," he said to his cup. "There are no

bubbles to interrupt the sounds of the sea. There's no awkward tank to get in your way. You can glide up and down through the water without worrying about decompression sickness or air use. You don't have to play around with putting the right amount of air in your vest." He looked into her eyes, and she was struck anew by the otherworldly paleness of his irises boring into hers. "It's like being on land, but so much better. There's no gravity, there's only you and the water surrounding you. Water currents flow over your skin, you taste the salt on your lips, you notice your heartbeat in the muffled quiet, and there is only calming green in front of your eyes. It's like nothing else."

That was the longest speech Zeb had ever said in front of Corrie. She was mesmerized by his description, his voice sliding into her ears like honey, and by his pale eyes staring into hers. She knew what it was like underwater, since she scuba dived plenty, but the way Zeb described it made her realize how much she was missing. She wanted to dive into the waves and experience the water the way Zeb did.

Zeb held her gaze for a moment longer, then he broke eye contact and shook himself out of the spell. Corrie blinked at the release and shivered. Raucous laughter rose from the corner, and Zeb looked over at Jules.

"I should probably drag Jules to the boat before he can't walk himself there," Zeb said.

"Yes," said Corrie distractedly. "Sure. Thanks so much for coming." She didn't know why she had reacted the way she had. Was it the bizarre thought of swimming in the freezing ocean that fascinated her, or was Zeb just a good storyteller? The uncertainty distressed her, so she took refuge in hostess platitudes. "It was great to see you. Take care of yourself with the goons, okay? And I'll email you when I get more data back."

It took a while for Zeb to drag Jules to his feet and say their goodbyes. Jules finally stumbled down the stairs, supported by Zeb, and Trip disappeared down the hall. Adrianna bid Corrie goodnight and pulled an unresisting Patrick to her bedroom downstairs.

Corrie put extra pizza in the fridge and straightened pizza boxes. Leaving an untidy kitchen didn't work for her. David half-heartedly helped, although she knew he was waiting for her to be done.

"What did you think?" Corrie asked while she placed the leftover wine in a cupboard.

"Pizza was good," said David. "I like that place better than my usual one. Less greasy."

Corrie sighed but tried to keep her exasperation out of the sound.

"No, I meant what did you think of Zeb and Jules?"

Corrie wasn't sure what she wanted out of that question. It was clear that David had some beef about Zeb. Maybe she wanted to get it out in the open. Maybe she wanted to hear David's justifications for his behavior. Maybe she wanted to pick a fight. David answered calmly, as he usually did.

"Jules is a drinker but decent enough, from what I could tell. Trip monopolized him most of the evening. Zeb's an uptight slacker. Weird combo, but there you are."

Corrie bristled.

"He was only uptight because you were being weird."

David stared.

"Being weird? What are you talking about?"

"You were practically interrogating him, judging his life choices, making him uncomfortable. Why would you do that?"

"I was conversing with a guest," David said stiffly. "I don't know what you're talking about. I'm sorry if you thought I was 'being weird,' but I assure you there was no intention to make Zeb feel uncomfortable."

Corrie tapped her fingers on the counter. Now that she'd started this conversation, she couldn't back out. It was time to air this laundry and figure out what David's problem was.

"What's the real issue here?" she asked. "You've been weird about my trip on the boat and everything and everyone connected with it. Are you jealous? Do you think I'm going behind your back and cheating on you with Zeb?" There, it was out. She'd said it, and it felt good to bring it to the front. Corrie didn't like subtext and insinuations. David might be prepared to hold a grudge and nurse his issues, but Corrie needed them on the table and dealt with. She brought out the big guns. "Is that the kind of woman you think I am?"

"What?" David was clearly horrified at the turn that this conversation had gone. "No, of course I trust you. There's—" He rubbed his forehead with his fingers and thumb. "You know what, maybe I did feel a little jealous, but only in the back of my mind. You're so beautiful, so wonderful, that I can't imagine you wanting to stick with me." He reached out and held her hands with a soulful look into her eyes. "Sometimes I can't think straight about you. I'm sorry."

Corrie stared at him. It was a good apology, no doubt about it. It sounded reasonable and sincere. He probably believed it himself.

"I don't have much patience for jealousy, you'll find," she said. It was smart to make her stance clear. It would save her hassle in the future. "It reeks of control, which I won't tolerate."

"I'm sorry," he said, looking truly chastened. "I'll do better in the future, I promise."

Corrie wavered, then decided that he'd repented enough. She stood on her tiptoes and kissed his lips. He responded fervently, as if he realized how close he had been to losing her. They retired to Corrie's bedroom, where David showed Corrie exactly how sorry he was.

It wasn't until David was asleep beside her that Corrie examined her feelings. A part of her was slightly disappointed that he hadn't brought more fight to their argument. If he had gotten angry and justified his actions, it would have given her a reason to break up with him.

The thought surprised her. Was that what she wanted, really? Did she want David or not? What was she doing in bed with him if she felt that way?

She glanced at his sleeping face, and warm feelings washed over her. He did truly care for her. She didn't know if it was only the hormones after intimacy kicking in, but she felt protective and caring toward him too. He was only human, after all. They all needed understanding and forgiveness sometimes.

She fell asleep with her hand on his chest, but green water and pale eyes haunted her dreams.

ZEBALLOS

Jules gazed out of the bus window at passing headlights in a dreamy stupor. Zeb glanced at him and shook his head with a half-smile. For the amount of time Jules spent inebriated, it was lucky that he was a happy drunk.

Zeb couldn't claim the same blissful state. He was faintly irritated, but by what he wasn't sure. The evening sat heavily in his stomach as though he'd eaten too much, although he'd only had three slices of pizza. Too much drink wasn't the issue—he'd nursed his two beers, unable to let down his guard with David hounding him. Jules would probably say that lack of drink was the problem, right there. He shifted in his seat, trying to get comfortable.

"What are you so fidgety for?" Jules asked. "Relax. It's late, we're coming back from drinks and dinner with new friends. Just chill, for once."

"Maybe I need a swim." As soon as Zeb said it aloud, though, he knew that wasn't the issue. A swim sounded pleasant, but not currently necessary.

"No, you're not rubbing your arms, like you do. This is different." Jules snapped his fingers. "I know what it is. You need to get laid."

"Shut up," Zeb said automatically.

"No, seriously. We were at a house party with three pretty girls. It's only natural. Honestly, when was the last time?"

"I don't remember," Zeb said, but it wasn't true. His latest intimate encounter with the opposite sex had been with a beautiful woman named Amanda, who had joined her cousin on a diving charter tour helmed by Zeb's father. She had maneuvered herself into unlikely scenarios to get him alone, no small feat on a boat the size of the *Clicker*. Once he'd figured out what she was doing, his help made her machinations much more profitable.

"Don't give me that," Jules said. "You're no Casanova, you remember."

Zeb sent him a glare as a matter of course but replied reluctantly.

"She was a diver, a pretty brunette. Were you on that trip?"

"I remember. Big tits, giggled a lot." Jules leaned his head back in reflection. "That was months ago."

"You're one to talk. When was your last time?"

Zeb fully knew the answer, but the flash of irritation that Jules' reminder provoked in him had prompted his question.

"Carole," Jules said in the mournful groan of a bull sea lion.

Zeb didn't reply, already regretting the quick words that had hurt his best friend. They lapsed into silence. Headlights on the highway lit Jules' thoughtful face in an irregular staccato of light. Zeb's mind wandered to Amanda, but his fling with her seemed so long ago that it was almost dreamlike. Jules eventually broke the silence.

"What did you think of Trip?"

Zeb smiled to himself. Subtleness was the first trait that Jules lost when he was drunk, and it was clear where Jules' train of thought had come from. He and Trip had seemed to bond over their shared love of tequila, although Zeb hadn't been paying too much attention to their conversation, as engrossed in awkward exchanges with David as he had been.

"I didn't talk to her much," Zeb said truthfully. "But she seemed nice."

"Yeah." Jules sighed and gazed out the window.

Zeb looked out the front windshield, where the wipers flicked the rain back and forth, back and forth. He pulled his wallet out of his pocket and turned it around and around in his hands to give them something to do. He caught himself wondering what Corrie was doing right now and forced his thoughts away. That was far too complicated a path to consider exploring.

The bus dropped them at the top of a hill. A streetlight in the darkness highlighted falling rain that dampened Zeb's shirt. They walked down to the marina where the *Clicker* was tied up. Their walk was more of a toddling stumble in Jules' case, with Zeb guiding him around obstructions.

Zeb managed to stop Jules from falling over the dock's edge, although he wondered if the shock of cold seawater would be enough to sober him up, and he was partly tempted to try. It wasn't like Jules would be in any danger, not with Zeb to fish him out. He resisted and instead pulled Jules over the bulwark and into his cabin.

Jules fell into his bunk without undressing and was snoring before Zeb left the room. Zeb shook his head and wondered whether Jules would ever grow out of the habit of excess. It was difficult to imagine.

He wandered to the galley, his stomach still heavy and unsettled. As a matter of course, he reached to the top cupboard and extracted a piece of jellyfish from the now always-open bag. He leaned against the counter and chewed the piece. His mind drifted. Visions danced before him of the graceful ligan, steaming pizza, pulsing jellyfish, the sparkles of Corrie's low-cut shirt, David's smug smile…

Zeb shook his head and walked to the deck. His brain was not cooperating. Maybe some fresh air would help. His eyes raked over the nearby boats, looking for details to distract himself from the confusing evening.

A new motorboat gleamed in the pale moonlight. Zeb squinted to read the name on the bow.

Discoverer.

Zeb cursed. How had the goons found the *Clicker* already? There were plenty of marinas around.

The *Discoverer* was dark and quiet. Maybe the goons were

asleep and would continue their nefarious plans in the morning, by which time he and Jules would be gone. Zeb nodded with decision and turned to the cabin door.

He was still too fidgety to sleep. Maybe a swim would feel good, even though it likely wasn't the cause of his disquiet. He walked to the galley and ripped a piece of loose paper off a notebook that was tucked into a pouch on the wall. He scrawled a note to Jules in the rare case he woke up in the next hour.

Zeb tucked it under a cutting board in the galley, where Jules was likely to find it. Then he took off his clothes, his trusty swimsuit underneath as always, and slipped outside to grab his flippers.

He had ten glorious seconds of cool water sliding unfettered over his skin in the darkness of the night ocean. He opened his senses to feel his surroundings, but too late.

His face smashed into a barrier of crisscrossed rope. His fingers pushed through, but his hands were too large to fit through the holes. He thrashed backward to get away from the ropes, not understanding what it was. His back hit the same ropes, then his flailing feet. Finally, he understood. He was caught in a net.

He pushed against the net with wilder motions, but it only tightened around him. Water flowed through the net and over his skin as the net was towed forward. Zeb's heartbeat sped up to land speed. He pulled himself toward the front of the net, hoping to find a hole where he could escape, but the net jerked upward. He fell against the bottom, limbs twisting painfully around his torso as the net was hauled into the air. He swung in his rope prison above the sea.

"Freshly caught," said a man to Zeb's right. Zeb strained to look at the speaker on the fishboat nearby. "Funny haul today. What do you think, catch and release or bag it?"

Another man chuckled.

"Bring him in. He's the one we want."

A winch started up, and Zeb's net was brought closer to the deck where the two men stood. Zeb readied himself. When the winch laid him on the deck, Zeb clawed the net open and tried to rise. Something struck him in the back and his whole body seized with immobility and pain.

"Got to love these tasers," one of the men said with satisfaction, before Zeb's vision faded to black.

JULES

Jules woke up then wished he hadn't. His sleep had been fragmented and his dreams ridiculous, but at least his head hadn't been split in half by a particularly vindictive lumberjack. He groaned aloud and regretted the noise as soon as it came out of his mouth, because the lumberjack gave a shout of joy and swung his ax with greater fervor.

Jules took a deep breath and rolled out of bed with one swift motion. The room spun in a sickening way but righted itself before his stomach decided to revolt. He carefully rose to his feet, noting that he was still dressed in last night's clothes, and stumbled out of his cabin.

Once in the galley, he gulped a glass of water while he waited for the kettle to boil. His eyes were barely open, and he was grateful that he knew the galley well enough to make coffee by feel.

"Come on, come on," he whispered, willing the water to boil faster. He wondered how bad instant coffee tasted straight from the jar and decided he could wait a few minutes. Probably. He'd give it a minute and reassess.

When steam finally billowed out of the kettle's spout, Jules lunged forward and poured water into a waiting mug. Heedless of the temperature, Jules sipped the coffee and smiled. It probably looked more like a grimace, were anyone watching, but it was a beam of gratitude from Jules this morning.

Three cups of coffee and a piece of dry toast later, and Jules felt well enough to wonder where Zeb was. It was unlike him to sleep in, and he hadn't looked as drunk as Jules last night. Of course, Jules hadn't been in a state to assess, so it was possible Zeb was now nursing a hangover to end all hangovers.

By the time the galley clock struck noon, however, Jules decided he was bored. He shuffled to Zeb's cabin and stuck his head in.

"Come on, you lazy—" he started, then his voice tailed off. The upper bunk was filled with strapped-down cardboard boxes, and the lower bunk was empty and still covered with the clothes Zeb had discarded in his quest to appear presentable at Corrie's house.

Had Zeb not slept last night? Jules prowled around the boat, but Zeb was nowhere. There wasn't anything interesting within walking distance, so it was unlikely he'd left the boat on foot. Jules moved back to Zeb's cabin, but his phone and wallet were on the top of the chest of drawers. He checked behind the life ring for Zeb's flippers, but they were gone.

Jules wandered back to the galley. His eye was drawn to the note tucked under the cutting board. How had he missed it earlier?

Gone for a swim. We'll leave early tomorrow—the goons are in this marina.

That explained the flippers gone, but not the unslept-in bed, nor the fact that they weren't underway, and it was past noon. Either Zeb went for a swim last night, in which case he'd been gone for too long, or he went this morning, but for some reason didn't sleep in his bed. Something didn't add up.

Jules went to the deck and looked around for the *Discoverer*. It wasn't anywhere in sight. His mind, still slow from his hangover, thought about the goons, and his uneasy stomach tightened. The goons wanted answers. Could they have taken Zeb? The thought was too horrible to consider, but the longer Jules thought about it, the more likely it seemed. The goons knew about Zeb's swimming abilities, and they had probably been lying in wait for him to dive in. Miles Callahan wanted answers, and he thought Zeb had them. Jules' lungs suddenly felt too small for the air he needed.

He ran to his cabin and grabbed his phone.

"Corrie," he gasped when she answered. "It's Jules. They've taken Zeb."

CORRIE

Corrie typed on her computer in the living room. Her supervisor was at a conference this week and wouldn't notice if she worked from home today. Corrie liked to take advantage of the small mercies in life, especially after her late night. David had left early that morning for work, and Trip had dragged herself out of the house with numerous curses and black looks at anyone breathing too loudly. Adrianna, although volunteering at a wildlife rehabilitation center in the morning, had come home for lunch to prepare for her afternoon classes, and was currently in the kitchen, rummaging in the fridge.

Corrie could be doing more lab work—goodness knows, she had enough of it—but data analysis was important, too. How would she know if her methods in the lab were working, if she didn't check the data occasionally? That it just so happened to coincide with a late night was a happy coincidence. She'd earned a minute to put her feet up, with all the lab work and field work she'd done in the past few weeks.

Her phone rang, and for one horrified moment, she thought it might be Jonathan, checking up on her. When the screen said Jules, she breathed easier. Her supervisor was not omniscient, as much as she feared it. She answered with a happy smile in her voice.

"Hello."

"Corrie," Jules said. He sounded close to panic, and Corrie's heart clenched. "It's Jules. They've taken Zeb."

"What?" Corrie gasped. "What do you mean?"

"The goons' boat was here last night, Zeb noticed it. When I woke up, Zeb wasn't here, his bed wasn't slept in, and the goons' boat was gone. They took him, I know it."

"Did they come aboard?" Corrie, said, trying to inject some reason into this terrifying conversation. "Surely, you would have heard it."

"I think they got him when he was swimming," Jules blurted out. At Corrie's questioning silence, he said, "He, um, free dives. Maybe he went last night, I don't know. Or maybe they got him on the boat, and I was too drunk to wake up."

"Okay." Corrie breathed deeply. "It doesn't matter how it happened. We know who has him, and who's behind it. Come to my house. We'll make a plan. We'll get Zeb back."

There was a pause.

"Thanks, Corrie." Jules' voice was gruff, as if he were close to tears. "I'll be there soon."

Corrie stared at her phone for a long while after she hung up. Her mind whirled with useless panic. What could they do to get Zeb back? How would they even start? Should Corrie call the police? Corrie had no evidence for her suspicions, and she couldn't imagine the police having anything helpful to say. She didn't want to wade through red tape for hours, not when she knew who had taken him. Her blood boiled at the thought of Miles' smug face. She couldn't believe she had ever thought him charming.

Zeb's pale eyes, frightened in her mind's vision, flashed before her. She swallowed. There had to be a solution. She just hadn't thought of it yet.

Adrianna came into the living room and flopped onto the couch across from Corrie's armchair.

"It's lunchtime, and you work too hard," she said around a bite of her sandwich. "So, I'm going to talk to you for a few minutes." Adrianna noticed Corrie's grim face, and her smile slid off to be replaced by an expression of concern. "What's wrong, Corrie?"

"Zeb," Corrie whispered. She cleared her throat. "Zeb's missing. He's been kidnapped."

"What?" Adrianna blanched. "How do you know? You said he was rich, was there a ransom note?"

Corrie shook her head.

"There were clues. Jules is sure. And—" Corrie hesitated,

but what was the point of keeping secrets when spreading the word might save Zeb? Adrianna knew Miles, after all. She could have some insight that was eluding Corrie right now. "He was being followed by Tangled Net. They think he knows something about the unicorn fish, and they want him to talk. They beat up the last guy who they wanted information from, so I'm really worried."

Corrie passed a shaking hand over her eyes. This was serious. When had she turned from a scientist to someone who dealt with torture and kidnappings? What had her life turned into?

"Are you saying Miles Callahan abducted Zeb?" Adrianna voice was disbelieving. Corrie didn't respond, but she watched the expression on Adrianna's face change from disbelief to understanding as she thought. Corrie nodded.

"He's interested in one thing only: getting the newest and greatest first. Morals aren't his forte. How do you think he earned all that money? It wasn't with his magazine."

"No," Adrianna said faintly. "No, I've heard the rumors. Patrick always discounts them, he loves Miles. But there are too many to ignore."

"And now Zeb is gone. And if Miles has no misgivings about doing what needs to be done to get the information he wants, what's in store for Zeb?" The scent of Adrianna's sandwich turned Corrie's queasy stomach. She wanted to do something to help, instead of sitting here with a tumultuous mind, but she didn't know in what direction to turn.

Adrianna's mouth twisted in her concern.

"What can I do to help?"

"You believe me that Miles took Zeb?"

"You believe it, so I do, too. I trust you. But do you really think they would hurt Zeb? They probably just want to ask him questions."

"Who abducts someone just for a chat? And they beat up someone else I know, for the same information. But why did they take Zeb, instead of extracting the info on the boat?" Corrie jiggled her leg in thought. "What do they think Zeb has?"

Adrianna shrugged helplessly.

"What can we do?"

Corrie sat up straight. Determination flooded her system.

"I can go get him."

Adrianna looked skeptical.

"You mean, get a boat and drive to the island? Do you think he'll let Zeb go if you ask nicely?"

"Sure, I can ask nicely at first." Corrie narrowed her eyes. "Then I can ask not nicely."

"Do you have a hidden talent in karate that I don't know about?" Adrianna looked Corrie over. "Are you small but mighty?"

"You'd be surprised," Corrie said, thinking of the battle with Matt and Sucker. "I'm sure we could figure something out."

"Against professionals? I don't know exactly what Tangled Net does, but I'm guessing if they're in the shadier side of the security business, they can handle themselves."

Corrie sighed explosively.

"I have to do something. I can't leave Zeb there, at the mercy of Miles and his goons."

"We have to do something, you mean." Adrianna gave Corrie a look of defiance. "I'm coming, too."

"This isn't your fight," Corrie said in surprise. "And Patrick works for Miles. It could get awkward."

"Let me deal with Patrick."

Corrie's throat tightened. It was good to know that Adrianna had her back. They'd been friends for less than a year, after all. Adrianna's loyalty wasn't something Corrie took for granted.

"We should wait for Jules," she said finally. "He's the one with the boat. And he might have some ideas."

Adrianna stood up.

"I need to phone one of my classmates, ask him to take notes for me this afternoon. I'll keep an ear out for the door." She walked to her bedroom with her sandwich forgotten on the table.

Corrie picked up her own phone. Had Jules called Krista? She'd better do it, just in case. Krista would want to know about Zeb's disappearance. Corrie gritted her teeth and dialed Krista's number. She hated giving bad news, but she hated the thought of Krista not knowing more. Corrie knew that she would want to know, if her own sibling had been abducted.

Krista picked up on the fourth ring.

"Make it quick, Corrie. I have a lot to do."

"Zeb's been abducted by the goons," Corrie blurted out. There was silence on the line.

"What the hell are you talking about?" Krista said faintly after a long pause.

"Jules is certain. The goons' boat was in the marina last night, and now it's gone. So is Zeb. Jules figures they took him while he was swimming last night, although I don't know why anyone would free dive in the dark. I know Zeb has amazing navigation skills, but still." Corrie felt herself start to babble in her stress. With a great effort, she reined herself in to the important details. "Jules is coming over now. We're going to come up with a plan to get Zeb back."

Krista let out a long, low curse.

"I told him to be more careful. Why didn't he listen? He's such a stubborn ass. Damn it. What can I do?" Krista sounded close to panic. Corrie felt alarmed at confident Krista unraveling. "I can't do anything from here."

A faint hope crossed Corrie's mind.

"Krista, listen. You said you knew something about Miles Callahan, something shady about him. That's who is behind all this. We need some way to get him to stop going after Zeb and the fish. Can you find any dirt on him for leverage?" She took a deep breath. "Beyond summoning Sucker again, I don't know how to fight Miles and his goons. We need to be smarter, not stronger.”

“Maybe. I can try.” Krista’s wavering voice strengthened. “And if I can’t, I’m finding Miles and beating him up personally.”

Despite the situation, Corrie smiled.

“Hopefully, it won’t come to that. We’ll do our best from here. Let me know if you find anything.”

KRISTA

Krista leaned against the wall of the hallway at work. Her stomach, while steady enough to endure the roughest seas, churned at Corrie's news. Zeb was missing. Her little brother had gone somewhere she couldn't protect him, taken by someone she didn't know how to get at.

At this thought, Krista's blood grew hot and her teeth clenched until her jaw ached. Miles Callahan. He was behind this. He was steamrollering anything in his path to get the information he wanted, never mind the collateral damage. It was under his orders that Zeb was now caught like a fish in a net, unable to free himself.

Her stomach cramped at a vision of Zeb, a prisoner in a dark basement, trapped. The cold wouldn't bother him, but what if he couldn't swim? What would he do? If they really wanted information, depriving him of the ocean was the best torture. Krista shivered. How much did they know, anyway? What did they want from him?

What would they find out about Zeb?

She needed ammunition, something that would hurt Miles right to the core. She wanted to rescue Zeb then punish Miles. There was so little she could do from here, even though she wanted to squeeze Miles' neck until he turned purple. She could go to the police, but with no evidence, their hands would be tied, even if she could convince someone.

Krista had never felt so powerless. It was a terrible feeling, and she wracked her brain to find a way to change the situation. There had to be something she could do to help.

Corrie had suggested looking up dirt on Miles Callahan. Krista straightened. She could do that. He was a public figure with his fingers in many pots. Surely, some of his indiscretions were uncoverable. She simply had to work harder to find them. She was good at working hard. She would start now and hang her real work. There was all evening to do that. Her brother was more important.

"Krista, there you are." Her colleague Fiona stopped in front of her. "Have you eaten yet? A few of us are going for a late lunch downstairs. I'm starving."

"Not today, thanks, Fiona," Krista said automatically. She cast around for an excuse. "I'm not feeling great."

Fiona peered into her face.

"You do look a bit peaky. Are you sure a quick bite won't settle you?"

"Yes, I'm sure."

When Fiona shrugged and turned to go, Krista had a brainwave.

"Fiona, I overheard you asking around about Miles Callahan. Did you find anything interesting?"

Fiona looked back with a coy smile.

"You think I'm going to divulge juicy gossip in the hallway? Not a chance. The only way I'll spill the beans is if you join me on a girls' outing." Fiona clicked her fingernails against her purse. "Gossip this good needs a really girly activity. I know." She pointed a finger at Krista. "You come and get your nails done with me, and I'll tell you everything."

Krista's distaste must have shown on her face, because Fiona laughed.

"That's my price," she said with a wave. She turned. "Feel better soon, Krista."

Krista shook her head. It was doubtful Fiona knew anything useful. Krista needed solid evidence, some shady dealings that she could point to and use as leverage. Gossipy hearsay wouldn't do Zeb any good. Fiona could keep her girly chats and her nail polish. Krista was going to save her brother her way.

JULES

Jules stepped off the bus and strode in the direction of Corrie's house. His stomach churned from guilt, fear for Zeb, and hangover-induced nausea. Who knew how long Zeb had been in the hands of the goons? Possibly all night.

Jules was supposed to have kept an eye on Zeb. He'd promised Krista, and he'd promised himself. He'd let his guard down for one stinking night, and now Zeb was gone. Jules had failed his friend. He had known the stakes, known the danger, and he'd still messed up.

His uselessness threatened to overwhelm him. What could he do? He hoped Corrie had some brilliant ideas, because he couldn't think of any. His mind was fuzzy from the hangover, and he wasn't a thinker at the best of times. Krista had certainly reminded him of that often.

At the house, Jules knocked loudly. A moment later, Corrie threw the door open wide and flung her arms around him. She was soft and warm and would have felt wonderful if he had deserved the sympathy. He gently disengaged from the embrace.

"Come in, come in," Corrie said, ushering him forward. "Let's figure this out."

Jules walked up the stairs with heavy feet and was surprised to see Adrianna in the living room with a concerned expression on her face.

"Hi," he said. "Sorry to interrupt."

"Don't be silly, we were waiting for you," she said. "We need to figure out how to get Zeb back. Three heads are better than two."

Jules let out his breath in a sigh of relief. His useless brain wasn't coming up with any bright ideas, but with these two smart women on the task, they would think of something.

"I'm glad you're here," he said. He sunk into an armchair

and spread his hands. "I need all the help I can get."

Corrie followed him and tucked a foot under her as she sat on the couch. Adrianna remained standing.

"Remind me again why they took Zeb?" Adrianna asked. Jules looked at Corrie in a panic. What should he say? What did Adrianna know, and what should she know? He was just the cook and deckhand on this creature-hunting expedition. He didn't make any of the important decisions.

Corrie waved her hand.

"Adrianna knows everything, don't worry."

"That makes things simpler." Jules rubbed his face while he thought of what to say. It wasn't easy to distill this mess into a few coherent sentences. "Miles Callahan thinks that Zeb knows something about the unicorn fish. He sent the goons after us to find out more. I guess they didn't find what they wanted, so they nabbed Zeb instead."

Adrianna whistled.

"Right. That's messed up. Okay, what are our options? Police?"

"Too slow," said Corrie at once. "We have no real evidence that Miles is behind it. Their hands would be tied."

"And you're sure he was taken?" said Adrianna to Jules. "He didn't fall off the boat, or wander away, or something? I believe you, I promise, but we need to rule out all options."

"He was taken," said Jules firmly. There was no doubt in his mind. The note, the made bed, the *Discoverer* gone—it all added up to one conclusion. Zeb didn't wander away on foot, as the note proved, and he would have been fine if he had fallen off the boat. "The clues are watertight. I'm one hundred percent sure."

Adrianna nodded.

"Okay, that's good enough for me."

"It was the goons, and Miles is behind them," said Corrie with surprising venom. "If you were Miles, where would you take someone who you'd recently abducted?"

"That's not a question I've ever had to ask myself," Jules said. His attempt at humor only twisted his stomach into a tighter knot. "What do we know about him?"

"He has no ties to Victoria that I know of," Adrianna said. "His base is in Vancouver, work and home both. The only other place is his private island."

"It's pretty obvious that he'd take Zeb there," said Corrie.

"They already have the boat, the *Discoverer*," said Jules, warming up to their discussion.

"And a private island is the definition of secluded." Adrianna started to pace. "And there's nowhere for prisoners to run."

That wasn't true in Zeb's case, but Jules didn't see any reason to divulge Zeb's secret. It didn't have any bearing on their rescue mission, and Zeb wouldn't thank him for being loose-lipped.

Adrianna stopped pacing and turned to them.

"This is stupid. I'm going to call Miles, see where he is." She slid her phone out of her jeans' pocket. "It's worth a try."

Jules waited with breath held while Adrianna listened to her phone. After a minute, she hung up with a disgruntled look.

"I guess that would have been too easy."

The three of them were silent for a long moment.

"We have to go to the island," Corrie said finally. "I can't think of anything else to do. Zeb is there, and he needs our help. No one else is going to ride in and save him. It's up to us."

Jules rested his head in his hands. He wished with all his heart and nervous stomach that this wasn't the only way. He felt boxed into the path of confrontation, and it was the path he always avoided. It was too bad Corrie and Adrianna hadn't come up with a cleverer way, but who was he to judge? It wasn't like he had thought of anything brilliant.

There was no other way. Jules didn't want to drive to this island and enter a dangerous fray, but Zeb was there. The thought of Zeb tied up, beaten and bloody, steeled Jules' resolve. Zeb needed him. He could do this. He would have to.

"We can take the *Clicker* there," he said when he lifted his head. "It's gassed up and ready to go."

"I can drive us to the boat," said Adrianna. "Give me a few minutes to get ready."

She disappeared down the stairs. Corrie turned to Jules with a sympathetic look on her face. Jules wished she would stop doing that. It was his fault Zeb was gone. He didn't deserve her pitying looks.

"How are you doing, Jules?" she asked. "It must have been a shock, finding him taken."

"I feel terrible," he said. "And terrified. What are we going to accomplish on this island? We have to go, I'm not denying that, but what can we really do?"

"That's what I asked myself before our Sucker showdown," said Corrie with a faint smile. "And that turned out okay. We'll have to wing it."

As Jules had played only a minor, sidelined role in that skirmish, Corrie's pep talk didn't cheer him up as much as Corrie probably thought it would. Before he could reply, the doorbell rang. Corrie leaped to answer it. Patrick's voice drifted up the stairs.

"Hi, Corrie. Is Adrianna in? I thought I'd stop by for a quick lunch with her."

"She's in her bedroom," Corrie answered. "You know where it is."

Patrick laughed. His steps faded from hearing as he walked along the downstairs hallway. Corrie pattered upstairs.

"I'm going to get ready, too. Give me five minutes, okay?"

"No problem," Jules answered. Corrie disappeared down the hall.

Jules stared at the couch for a moment, but it provided neither comfort nor answers. He stood and followed his feet to the kitchen. Here, he leaned against the counter to wait. It might not be his kitchen, but it was better to be surrounded by the comfort of familiar scenery than to dwell on Zeb's disappearance in the living room.

ADRIANNA

Adrianna slipped into her nicer pair of jogging pants. They were comfortable, had lots of stretch, and made her butt look great. There was no point in ever looking drab if she could help it, even when jogging. And for this mission, she wanted to look good, just in case it came in handy. Looking good often did. It never hurt to be prepared.

What else would she need? Adrianna looked around her room, pondering what one took for a rescue mission. There was a knock on the door, and her boyfriend Patrick entered the room.

"Hi, gorgeous." He swooped in and kissed her on the lips. She smiled and twined her arms around his neck. He took this as an invitation to start nuzzling her neck. She let him for a minute, then she pulled away.

"No time for that today, I'm afraid. I'm heading out in a minute."

Patrick gave her a puppy-dog face, and she laughed.

"Where are you going? I thought class wasn't for another hour. I made a special trip to show you how much I love you." He gave her a winning smile. Adrianna brushed his cheek with her fingertips.

"Trust me, I appreciate it and would love to take you up on your offer. But I have to help Corrie with something. Do you remember her friend Zeb from last night?"

"Yes, of course. What about him?"

"He's been kidnapped," Adrianna said flatly. It still sounded bizarre. People weren't kidnapped in real life. This whole afternoon had a fog of unreality about it. The only thing she was clear on was Corrie's need. Her friend needed her, and she was there to help. It was simple.

"What?" Patrick looked perplexed. "Why?"

"They think he has information they want, and they're going

to get it out of him, no matter what."

"Has Corrie called the police?"

"There's only circumstantial evidence about who took him, although it really is clear."

"Who took him, then?"

Adrianna paused. She knew Patrick wouldn't like the answer, but they didn't keep secrets from each other, and she wasn't about to start now.

"Tangled Net."

Patrick's face went from puzzlement to incredulity.

"You're saying Miles Callahan kidnapped somebody? That's a big accusation."

"I don't say it lightly." Adrianna knew how much Patrick looked up to his boss. She didn't like pulling back the curtain on his hero, but she couldn't undo what Miles had done. "We're certain it's him."

"Now what?" Patrick spread his hands in doubt. "What's your plan? You ask Miles nicely to let Zeb go? You're not a trained hostage negotiator."

"Miles is a reasonable man." Adrianna wasn't at all sure of this, after what she had found out about him, but Patrick needed reassurance. "It's worth trying to talk. Maybe there's been some misunderstanding. You never know."

"I still find this hard to believe." Patrick rubbed the short curls of his dark hair into disarray. "You're absolutely certain Zeb isn't drunk in an alley somewhere? It wouldn't be the first time a missing person was only late coming home."

Adrianna bristled at the accusation against Corrie's friend, but she kept her tone calm. Patrick was grasping at straws, in denial about his boss' shady dealings. It was natural to put the blame elsewhere.

"We're sure."

"Come on, Addy." Patrick took her hand in both of his. "This is Miles we're talking about. He's my boss. We've been over to his house for lunch. He's a good guy."

"I agree, there might be a misunderstanding. This could have a perfectly rational explanation. But I need to go with Corrie to solve this confusion and get Zeb back."

Patrick rubbed her fingers, his look pleading.

"Please be tactful. He's my boss. You can't go accusing him, especially without proof."

Adrianna sighed. She knew Patrick was between a rock and a hard place, but she had firm views, and what was a conundrum to Patrick was quite simple to her.

"Corrie's friend might be in danger. I'll do my best not to burn any bridges, but Zeb's safety comes first."

Patrick let go of her hand, a hurt look crossing his face.

"Are you choosing Corrie over me?"

Indignation flared up in Adrianna's chest. How could he boil this conversation down into a competition? How did his standing with his boss even compare to what Zeb might be going through?

"I'm choosing a life over a job," she said stiffly. It might be a touch melodramatic—even now, she didn't believe Miles would stoop to murder, although beating up someone for information veered too close to that line for her comfort—but she needed to get her point across, since Patrick was having a hard time accepting it. "I'm sorry you don't understand. I promise I'll be careful and as diplomatic as I can be."

She swallowed her anger and kissed Patrick on the cheek. He didn't reciprocate, but he didn't shy away, either. Adrianna took that as a good sign. She didn't like being at odds with Patrick. They'd been together for over a year, now, and she was as certain about him as she'd ever been about anything in her life, but she wasn't about to relax her values for his comfort. She hoped he would understand, eventually.

Adrianna left the room. In the hallway was her work bag, dropped there when she had arrived home after work this morning. With a start, she recalled the two syringes of ketamine tucked in the bottom. She'd meant to replace the sedatives on the shelf at the wildlife center after an unsuccessful capture of a cougar, but they languished in her bag. She bent down and retrieved them. They slid into her jacket pocket easily. It never hurt to be prepared.

KRISTA

Krista rubbed her forehead. She'd been researching for two hours, fending off irate senior partners looking for completed tasks, and had found nothing. Miles Callahan was squeaky clean, on paper, at least. He'd been through the courts a few times but had been exonerated of all charges. His record was clean.

Krista ground her teeth. There had to be something else she could examine, or somewhere else she could look. She knew Miles wasn't the upstanding citizen that he portrayed, but she couldn't find anything to prove her convictions. She had nothing but the word of Matt Nielsen and hearsay about the origins of Tangled Net. It wasn't enough to convince Miles to let Zeb go, not nearly enough. Miles would laugh in her face, smug in the knowledge that he was untouchable, the way too many of these rich men were.

It galled Krista to her very core that Miles might get away with his crimes. This was the reason she had got into law in the first place, to bring justice to those who thought they were above it. She was failing the system, and she was failing Zeb. Her eyes pricked with tears, although she refused to let them fall. Tears didn't help solve anything, and they wouldn't help her find Zeb.

Maybe it wasn't such a big deal that Miles was questioning Zeb. Miles would ask about the unicorn fish, Zeb wouldn't say much, the goons might rough him up a bit then let him go. She might be worrying for nothing. Krista didn't think Miles was necessarily a killer.

Injury wasn't the only thing to worry about with Zeb, though. Miles wanted the enhancer from the unicorn fish. He thought Zeb knew something about it. Krista still didn't know how Zeb had scared off the goons underwater, but she had a shrewd suspicion that the goons had seen some unusual speed and underwater skills. At the very least, Zeb would have been without mask and wetsuit. If Miles thought Zeb was using the enhancer, he wouldn't stop until Zeb had told him everything about it.

And if they found out that Zeb's abilities didn't come from an enhancer? What would they do then? It was Krista's worst fear: Zeb being scrutinized in a cage. Zeb had often scoffed at her for being paranoid, but look who was caught now. Being right gave Krista no pleasure this time.

Miles must have taken Zeb to his island. It was the perfect private location to take someone for questioning. She was tempted to rent a speedboat from the nearest marina and race over there herself. The only thing stopping her was the knowledge that Miles was too smooth and careful. Hours of pouring over documents had taught her how good at hiding his trail he was. Brute force wouldn't work here, not like it had with Matt Nielsen. It was unfortunate—Krista was much better at storming fortresses than careful policy.

Despite her care, a tear escaped her eye and slid down her cheek. She didn't bother to wipe it away. Zeb was gone and there was nothing she could do to help.

Fiona's voice drifted through Krista's half-open door as she spoke to a colleague in the hall.

"You wouldn't believe it if I told you…"

The voice grew quieter as Fiona and the other person walked away from Krista's door.

There was one, last, faint hope available to Krista. She didn't have faith that it would bring her any closer to justice or bring Zeb back, but it was the only hope she had left. She dried her eyes with a decisive wipe, stood up tall, straightened her suit jacket, and marched to the door.

At an office three doors down, Krista knocked firmly.

"Come in," a bright voice answered.

"Hello, Fiona," Krista said, trying to inject some warmth into her tone. She was sure she failed miserably, but Fiona didn't seem to notice. She gave Krista an inquisitive smile.

"Krista, how are you? What can I help you with?"

Fiona was nosy, overly saccharine, and two-faced, but also genuinely caring. Krista willed the tears to stay down. She mustered up a return smile.

"Are you still interested in getting those nails done?"

Fiona stared at her in disbelief for a moment. Then she clapped her hands with childish delight and leaped up.

"Yes! I won you over." Fiona grabbed her coat off a wall hook and slung her purse over her shoulder. "It's been my personal challenge to get you out. Who knew it would be nails that would do it?" She winked at Krista.

"Well," Krista said. "I can't say that was the deciding factor…"

"I know. You want the dirt. I'm happy to oblige, whatever your reasons are. Come on, there's a place two blocks away."

"You're okay to go right now?" It was what Krista had hoped for but hadn't dared to dream. Time was crucial—who knew what Zeb was going through right now—but Fiona didn't know that. It was the middle of the afternoon, after all, and there was always so much to do. Fiona waved her hand airily.

"We have important things to discuss. It's a business meeting. Don't worry, no one's watching. You'll be fine with me. I can talk my way out of anything. Grab your things and let's go."

Outside the building, Fiona threaded her arm through Krista's. It was uncomfortable, as if they were reenacting a scene from a chick flick, but Krista rolled with it. Anything to make Fiona tell her secrets.

"Loosen up, Krista," Fiona said. "You're as stiff as a board. What's eating you? You seem even more tense than usual, and that's saying something."

"It's my brother," Krista said before she could stop herself. She bit the inside of her cheek in annoyance. Fiona clucked her tongue.

"Now we're getting somewhere. Younger or older? What's happening with brother dearest?"

"He's my younger brother—"

"I called that," Fiona said in a quiet voice to herself.

"And—" Krista didn't know what to say and cursed herself for opening her mouth. What had possessed her to say anything? She was supposed to be getting news from Fiona, not spilling her guts to the other woman. It was too late now, though. She had to say something. "He's missing. I can't get a hold of him, and neither can his friends. It feels too early to file a missing person report, but I know him. He wouldn't disappear like this."

"Oh, doll," Fiona said with sympathy. Krista tightened her lips. No one called her "doll," although it didn't sound terrible coming from Fiona. If they ever talked after this, Krista could correct her then. "That's rough. What do you think happened? Anywhere else you can look?"

"He's not even in the city, that's part of the problem. There's nothing I can do from here. I can't help."

Fiona squeezed her arm.

"It's terrible feeling helpless, isn't it? Try to trust in him— there might be a perfectly good explanation. If you haven't heard one by tomorrow, file that report. I'll take you to the station myself if you need me to."

Krista nodded. She didn't trust herself to speak. Fiona patted her arm briskly.

"You need a distraction," she said brightly. "And I have just the thing. I have absolutely shocking news about Miles Callahan. You will not believe what I dug up. All from irreproachable sources." She smiled wickedly. "Mr. Callahan has been a very naughty boy."

CORRIE

Corrie flew around her bedroom, finding clothes to wear and thinking hard about what she would need. What would they face on the island? Should she dress in a cute sundress and appeal to Miles' better side, slide into ninja clothes for a covert sneak-in, or don battle gear for a full-scale confrontation? She had no idea what to expect.

She could probably cross off battle gear, since her closet didn't have a supply of bulletproof vests, and the materials for the makeshift utility belt she'd constructed out of lab gear for her fight with Matt Nielsen weren't accessible at home. Besides, she had no real fighting skills and they would likely be facing trained professionals. It was a laughable suggestion that she would prevail in a situation like that.

Likewise, the sundress approach didn't sound reasonable. Anyone who kidnapped strangers for profit was unlikely to be swayed by a sultry smile and shapely legs.

No, they needed to be sneaky, so Corrie picked out her finest ninja gear. The best she could manage was dark-colored skinny jeans and a tight-fitting black shirt. The top was more revealing than she wanted for their mission, but it was her only black one. She threw a few sneaky poses at the mirror and nodded. It would do.

She met a serious-looking Adrianna at the top of the stairs. She was sensibly yet stylishly dressed in magazine-worthy exercise gear. Corrie sighed, reminded of Krista's outfit for their fight against Matt and Sucker. Once again, she'd chosen less than appropriate clothing.

"You look ready to go," Corrie said. Adrianna looked her over.

"Are we on a rescue mission or a date?"

"I'm in ninja—never mind," Corrie said.

Her phone rang, sparing her from further explanation. She

picked it up.

"Hello?"

"Corrie, it's Krista. Check your email."

"Um, okay. Wait, I'll put you on speakerphone." Corrie moved to the kitchen where Jules was. Adrianna followed, and footsteps on the stairs indicated Patrick's arrival. Corrie opened her email and looked at the documents that Krista had sent her. "We're in a hurry, about to leave for the boat. Can you tell me what exactly I'm looking at?"

"Documents a colleague of mine recently unearthed," Krista said. "I had to pull major strings to get these, they were insanely well-hidden. Miles is a crafty bastard and knows how to cover his tracks. There's evidence damning him on multiple fronts, the biggest ones being signed confessions from silenced employees and evidence of fraud. It's big, Corrie."

Corrie looked at the documents, then up at Adrianna and Jules. They looked at her with identical expressions of confusion and hope. Corrie was sure the same was mirrored on her face.

"That's awesome, thanks, Krista. But—umm, I'm not sure what to do with this information."

"I don't know, either." Krista's voice was tight. If Corrie didn't know better, she would have said the other woman was close to tears. "That's all I can do from here. I thought it might help. I can start proceedings, take him to court, but that won't help Zeb today."

"Krista, listen to me." Corrie infused her voice with authority and confidence. "We'll get him back. We're going right now, and we will do everything we can to bring him home. Okay?"

There was a long pause.

"Good luck," Krista said in a muffled voice, then she hung up. Corrie put the phone in her pocket and looked at the other two.

"Ready? We have a friend to rescue, and an evil tycoon to

thwart."

Corrie caught sight of Patrick in the doorway. His face was full of frowning confusion, and Corrie remembered that Miles was his trusted boss. She felt a pang of sympathy for him—it was never easy to see your heroes fall—but she steeled her resolve. She and the others were the only ones coming to stop Miles' criminal plans. Zeb was waiting.

ZEBALLOS

When Zeb came to, his arms and legs were bound together behind him. His shoulders strained uncomfortably in the unnatural position. Rough cloth covered his eyes and pulled tightly against his mouth, preventing him from making more than a muffled grunt. Textured floor grazed his cheek. His grogginess lifted rapidly with his increasing heartbeat. He tried to figure out where he was and what had happened.

What did he remember? Diving in the ocean, swimming into a net, being hauled aboard, hit with a paralyzing shot in the back, darkness. The goons must be behind this. The loud roar of a motorboat nearly drowned out his thoughts. He must be on board the *Discoverer*. Where were they going? Miles Callahan lived in Vancouver, according to Corrie. Were they traveling all the way there? Surely not.

Then Zeb remembered the private island that Corrie had mentioned. That must be where they were headed. It was quiet and secluded.

But what did they want with Zeb? If they wanted to know more about the strolias, why not approach him and ask? They asked Matt Nielsen—using their fists, but still—so why not him? What did they want?

"He's awake," a man yelled over the growl of the motorboat. "What do you want me to do with him?"

Zeb couldn't hear the answer, but it must have been, "Leave him alone," because for the rest of the trip, Zeb lay bound, gagged, and blindfolded. By the time the motor throttled down to a chortling purr, Zeb's fear had subsided into anger. He was irate, and ready to show anyone who asked questions what he really thought of them.

The engine died. Footsteps pounded, vibrating the floor under Zeb's head. He strained against his bonds, but they were as immovable as the first time he had tried.

"We'll have to untie his legs," said one man. "I'm not carrying him up those stairs. There must be a hundred of them. And he's no featherweight."

"Keep his arms bound," said the other man. "And Flint, don't let him escape. We've worked too hard for this, and he's a slippery devil."

"I remember," said Flint. "Give me a hand, Gavin, if you're so worried."

Twin exhales were released as the two men knelt to untie his bonds. Zeb tensed, ready to use any looseness to his advantage. When the men released his legs, Zeb kicked wildly. Flint cursed. A moment later, Zeb's head was cuffed against the floor. It made a dull, ringing sound, and Zeb saw stars behind his blindfold.

"Don't try that again," Gavin warned. "Flint has a rather short temper, and we have our orders. If you don't like them, you will have your chance to speak to management shortly."

Flint chuckled.

"Not that he's the sympathetic one here, but you can try. On your feet."

Zeb was hauled up roughly by the elbows. He could barely stand—his legs cramped with their too-long imprisonment—but the flat of a hand pushed him forward and he stumbled along. He nearly fell on his face when he tripped over the edge of the platform leading to the dock.

"This is ridiculous," Gavin said. "Take off his blindfold, or we'll never get there. He can't get away with his hands bound."

Fingers tugged at the back of Zeb's head and released the blindfold. Zeb squinted in the brightness of early sunrise, his eyes nearly overcome by the orange light. He hobbled forward. When his eyes adjusted enough to see wooden dock below his feet and green waves to his left, his feet wandered toward the sea of their own accord. He could figure out how to release his bonds underwater, maybe find a shell to rub against or a sharp rock. If he could jump in, he'd be free.

"Grab his arm," Gavin said sharply to Flint. "He's thinking about making a run for it."

"A swim for it," Flint guffawed, but he gripped Zeb's forearm with meaty fingers. Zeb's heart sank. From what he could see out of the corner of his eye, Flint was too sturdily built to easily shake off. Maybe there would be another opportunity soon.

Flint stuck to him like a limpet along the dock and up the stairs, and Zeb's shoulders sunk as he climbed away from the ocean. Now, he was a prisoner with no opportunity for escape, so far from the sea. He would have to take his chances with whatever came next.

Flint huffed beside him when they reached the final step, and even Zeb's strong legs felt warm with exertion.

"For all his money, why doesn't the boss install an elevator?" Flint gasped at Gavin, who dusted off his jacket.

"Perhaps he enjoys the exercise. Come, he wanted us to bring him to the main house."

It was an impressive building, all glass windows and wooden beams. Zeb didn't care for it much—it was too high up the cliff, away from the waves below. He preferred beachside. His own apartment was as close to the water as he could afford.

A man with carefully styled dark hair and tailored trousers sat on the expansive cedar patio, sipping a mug of coffee and gazing at the horizon. When they trudged nearer, Gavin cleared his throat quietly. The man turned and flashed them a wide smile full of very straight teeth.

"You made it. Well done. Bring him here." The man stood and beckoned the trio forward.

"Thank you, Mr. Callahan," said Gavin. "He hasn't made too much fuss yet."

"Good, good."

Miles Callahan surveyed Zeb with interest. Zeb was not usually modest, but he was acutely aware of being clothed only in his swimsuit. He was still wet from his swim, hours before, and he wondered what Miles made of that. The other man only nodded with satisfaction.

"I'm glad you could join us, Zeballos Artino. I am pronouncing that right? Correct me if I'm not."

Zeb maintained a stony expression. He didn't care what Miles called him, only that he had an answer for why Zeb was here.

"Why did you abduct me?"

"Such an ugly word, 'abduct.' Although apt, I suppose." Miles laughed and Gavin smiled politely. "I have questions for you. I hope you will answer them willingly."

"I have nothing to say to you," Zeb growled. Miles tutted.

"One chance to change your mind. Would you like to answer questions in comfort, on a couch with a cup of coffee? Or would you prefer a more traditional interrogation?"

Zeb felt his ire rise at the audacity of this man. Without thinking, he spat at Miles. The spittle landed at the other man's feet. Miles nodded, a disappointed look on his face.

"I was afraid you would say that. Flint, bring him into the house, please. It looks like our guest is a traditionalist."

Flint grinned and yanked Zeb's arm. He stumbled after the beefy man.

The patio doors were open to a huge room with couches and chairs strategically placed to best admire the view. A long dining table ran along one side, and a door was open at the back, affording a glimpse of bedrooms beyond.

Gavin opened a drawer in a china cabinet and extracted a folded plastic sheet. He pulled a dining chair to a central location, away from rugs, and draped the sheet over top. Zeb grew cold at the sight. What exactly were they planning to do with him that required such waterproofing preparation? Flint must have seen his grim expression, because he chuckled.

"Mr. Callahan likes to keep his chairs clean. If you don't talk, we'll need the covers."

Flint thrust him into the chair. The plastic stuck to Zeb's bare skin. Flint wrenched his arms over the back of the chair and tied them down, then moved to his feet. Zeb kicked at Flint but missed. Flint backhanded Zeb across the face. While Zeb recovered from the blow, face numb and eyes watering, Flint strapped down his legs and stood back.

Miles stood before him, silhouetted against the rising sun in the windows.

"My name is Miles. I'm a seeker of opportunities."

He paused to let Zeb respond, but Zeb had nothing to say to this man. He waited for Miles to get on with whatever he had planned, determined not to give him anything. Miles continued.

"I have it on good authority that there is a new product on the market. It's an enhancer, for speed and strength underwater. There are some side effects above water, but that's nothing a good test lab and clinical trials can't weed out." Miles spread his hands wide. "Think of the tremendous applications of such an enhancer. Commercial divers, the military—there are a lot of people who would pay good money to get their hands on something like this. And if the enhancer can be modified to be used above water, the possibilities are endless."

Zeb glared at him and broke his vow of silence.

"Why beat me and Matt up for info? Why not just ask?"

"Would you have told me?" Miles said. When Zeb was silent, Miles nodded. "Exactly. This method, while perhaps objectionable, is so much quicker. And when you deal with cutting edge technology, time is crucial. If I'm not the first on the block, I might as well not be on the block. So." Miles sipped his coffee. "Tell me everything about these fish, the ones that produce the enhancer. Leave nothing out. Matt Nielsen indicated that you knew more than you let on."

"I'm not telling you anything," Zeb ground out. Miles sighed then waved to Flint. The goon backhanded Zeb again, three times in succession. Pain bloomed on Zeb's left cheek, and his head pounded.

"And now?" Miles said. Zeb shook his head, wincing at the pain. Flint hit him again, and Zeb tasted blood in his mouth.

When Zeb remained silent, Miles looked at him for a long moment.

"I wonder what you're protecting," he said at last. "Either you're simply stubborn, or you have a good reason for silence. My employees saw you underwater, performing feats of strength and speed that were more than humanly possible." Miles leaned forward and put his hands on the armrests of Zeb's chair. The smell of stale coffee wafted into Zeb's nose. "Here's my theory: you have a supply of enhancer that you're dipping into, and you want to keep it all to yourself." He stood up again.

"More?" said Flint.

"No," said Miles. Flint looked crestfallen. "Take him to the basement. Give him time to consider his options. I think he'll find he has very few."

CORRIE

Adrianna slammed her car into the nearest parking spot in the marina, and they all flew down the ramp to the dock. Jules led the way to the *Clicker*. It was just as Corrie remembered it, and she felt a pang of nostalgia for that crazy week of sampling and creature-hunting.

There wasn't time to dwell on memories. She leaped aboard and followed Jules to the wheelhouse. He dug keys out of a drawer with shaking fingers. Corrie put her hand on his shoulder.

"Deep breaths, Jules," she said quietly. "We can do this."

He didn't look at her, but he nodded and inserted the keys in the ignition. The engine coughed to life.

"I'll untie the boat," said Corrie. "Hold on."

She squeezed past Adrianna and jumped onto the dock once more. The headline at the bow was tightly wound around the cleats, and it took her a minute to figure out how to untie it, but she persevered. The sternline was easier. She climbed aboard as the boat drifted away from the dock, and a surge of adrenaline pumped through her veins. She raced back to the wheelhouse.

Adrianna spread out a chart and looked at it carefully. Jules gave it a glance occasionally, but his focus was on navigating the maze of docks.

"There it is." Adrianna pointed at a small island among many in the Gulf Islands. Corrie bent over to see.

"Yes, Kurina Island. Definitely. The dock was on this side." Corrie pointed to the eastern edge of the island.

"Are we trying to sneak in, or are we knocking on the front door?" Jules asked. "Because it matters where we make land. We're not going to hide our entrance if we pull up at a dock. Where's the house? Where would they take Zeb?"

"The house overlooks the dock," Corrie said. "It's on a cliff on the east side. I assume they'd take him there?"

"Yes, besides the pool house and a guest cottage nearby, there aren't any other outbuildings," said Adrianna. She tapped the chart in thought. "I think he said there was a beach on the west side. Maybe we could go there. But where do we park this boat, and how do we get ashore?"

"We'll anchor it and use the dinghy." Jules looked more comfortable talking about plans that he understood, and he had more color in his face than before. Corrie breathed easier. It was difficult enough to keep her own anxiety in check, let alone Jules' as well.

They exited the breakwater and Jules leaned over to look at the chart. Corrie pointed at Kurina Island. Jules nodded.

"It should take us an hour, maybe less."

"That long?" Adrianna said. "I'm sure it was quicker in Miles' boat."

"And how many knots did rich Miles' speedboat go?" said Jules with a ghost of a smile. "A few more than the *Clicker*, I bet. We'll get there, though."

It was an excruciatingly long hour. Corrie watched islands pass at a sluggish pace. Her leg jiggled at the delay. What were they doing to Zeb now? She didn't know Miles' endgame. Zeb knew who Miles was. Would Miles kill him after he'd got the information he wanted?

Her blood grew cold at the thought. Surely not. Miles couldn't be that heartless, that evil. She thought of his handsome, duplicitous face and shivered. She didn't know what people were capable of, not anymore. If he could order Matt's beating and abduct Zeb, what would stop him from carrying on? His moral compass was clearly malfunctioning or nonexistent.

"We're almost there." Jules broke the silence that they had descended into. Not even Corrie had thought of anything to say in the face of their next steps. She used Jules' words to break her out of her silence.

"Okay," she said. "We need a plan. Adrianna, where do you think Zeb would be? And how do we sneak up there and release him?"

"I've only been here twice," Adrianna said, but she straightened at the question. "There's a guest cottage and the pool house, which are possible locations and worth checking out. There shouldn't be anyone in them, so we can be sneaky and have a quick peek. Let's do that on the way up from the beach. If Zeb is there, we can quietly grab him and escape to the dinghy."

"Assuming there are no guards," said Jules.

"Then we distract the guards," said Corrie. "Somehow."

"In-the-moment planning," said Jules. He gave Corrie an amused look. "Is it your signature move?"

"I do my best," Corrie said in defense. Jules put up a hand.

"Trust me, I don't have any better suggestions. Carry on."

"If he's not there," Adrianna continued. "Then he's probably in the house. Since it's the middle of the day, our best bet is to enter via the bedrooms."

Corrie buried her head in her hands, overwhelmed by the enormity of what they were doing.

"This is insane, isn't it?" she whispered. Adrianna looked grim, but Jules looked at her squarely.

"Is it any more insane than summoning a giant octopus?"

Corrie released a breath of laughter. Jules was right. Sucker was far more insane.

"Point to Jules. All right, once we're in the house we sneak around until we find Zeb, distract again if necessary. Light a match under the fire alarm or something. Okay?"

Adrianna and Jules nodded with their eyes wide but determined. Corrie had never felt so underprepared for anything in her life, and that included a statistics exam in undergrad for which she hadn't studied, hadn't attended half of the classes, and was hungover. It hadn't gone well.

The island slid into view from behind another, larger island.

Corrie swallowed at the sight of the looming forest. It looked rugged and forbidding, not welcoming in the slightest. A wide rocky beach spanned the western edge, and Jules pointed the bow directly for it. There was a small dock jutting into the bay. It wasn't large enough for the *Clicker*, but it was suited for tying up the dinghy.

When they were shallow enough, Jules put the boat into neutral.

"I'm going to drop anchor," he said to Corrie. "When I wave at you, pull this lever a tiny bit until I wave again, okay? It will reverse the boat to set the anchor."

"Okay." Corrie looked at the lever with misgiving, but she nodded with a show of confidence. Jules swung out of the wheelhouse and started the windlass to release the anchor. Adrianna looked sideways at her.

"Ahoy there, captain."

Corrie grinned.

"Learn a new thing every day, right?"

"Transferable skills for your resume," Adrianna said.

They anchored without difficulty and put the dinghy in the water. There was no sign of life on the island, for which Corrie was thankful. If they were spotted now, what would they do?

Jules brought the dinghy up to the dock with a low roar then cut the engine. Corrie was struck by the silence of the scene, broken only by a chorus of waves splashing the rocky beach.

"No one has seen us yet," she said quietly, trying to install some confidence in her friends. Adrianna's face was grim, and Jules looked like he might vomit. Corrie was feeling far from confident herself—if Jules brought up his lunch, she might join him—but as self-appointed ringleader of their little band, she had to walk the walk. "Let's go before they do."

She hopped out of the dinghy and strode down the dock. There were hesitant steps on the wooden slats behind her, but she didn't look back. Her focus was on a narrow path between bushes that entered the woods in the center of the shoreline. It wasn't a large island. Chances were that the path led to Miles' house. She walked straight to it.

Once on the path, Corrie felt more secure because of the shelter of the trees, and more vulnerable because the sound of crashing waves didn't mask the noise of their feet on the twig-strewn path. She tried to walk carefully, but every so often a crack would resound through the woods, sounding like a cannon to Corrie's overwrought ears.

"What was that?" Adrianna hissed behind her. Corrie froze. She'd heard it too—a loud rustling noise from around a large bush masking their view of the path forward.

Corrie leaped to the side as quietly as she could and hid behind a tree. Adrianna and Jules followed her, and the three of them panted quietly together in wide-eyed panic.

A long moment later, an albino peacock shuffled out of the bush. It pecked at the path then sauntered toward the beach. Corrie nearly melted in her relief. Jules quietly chuckled.

"We're all a little wired," Adrianna said.

"Can you blame us?" said Corrie. "Come on, we won't find Zeb behind this tree. Let's face those peacocks head-on."

The rest of the short path passed by without alarm, although Corrie was sweating from nerves by the time a roof emerged through the trees. She slowed.

"There's the guest cottage," Adrianna whispered. "Let's peek in the windows."

They sneaked to the back of the cottage and peered in a window. There was a made bed, a dresser, and little else. A side window revealed an empty living area and kitchenette. There was no one on the front porch.

"One place down," Jules said. "Damn, I was hoping he'd be here, and we could grab him and run."

"Me, too," said Corrie. "Let's check the pool house."

Although the pool building was in a clearing with a direct line to the open cliff's edge, it stood between them and the main house. They ran to the back wall, which had no windows.

They stared at each other for a minute.

"Now, what?" Jules said at last. Corrie jiggled her leg while she thought.

"I'll have to go for it," she said. "Stay here. No point in all of us being seen if there's someone there. I'll peek in the windows. The whole two sides are windows, after all. It should be quick."

Before the others could protest, Corrie dipped around the side. She felt horribly exposed, although no one was on the main house's patio. She walked confidently along the walled side until she reached the corner where the windows started. She poked her head around.

"Whoa," a man said loudly.

Corrie's heart almost burst from her ribcage. The man was about her age and held a bucket of what looked like grout in one hand. He looked at her inquisitively.

"Can I help you?" he said.

Corrie thought with lightning speed. Then, she pasted on a huge smile and puffed out her chest.

"Yes, please," she said in a voice dripping with relief. "I just got here, but no one was at the dock. Miles said someone would greet me." She placed a light hand on the man's forearm and leaned in. "I know there aren't many places to look, but I didn't want be snoopy. Do you know where Miles is right now?"

The man smiled at her after a quick glance at her chest.

"Of course. It's a bigger island than it looks. I'm not sure where Mr. Callahan is—I'm just fixing the tiles in the pool—but he's probably in the main house, right there." He pointed. "I don't think he'd mind you knocking on the door."

"No, you're right." Corrie giggled. "Silly me. I'd better go see where he is. Thank you so much for your help." She squeezed his arm and let go. A quick glance at the pool as she turned showed her no sign of Zeb. She strutted slowly away, her heart hammering, and walked to the main house. When she turned, the man had his back to her and knelt over the edge of the pool. She ran to the back of the house, away from the patio and its menacing bank of windows, and crouched down below a bedroom window.

A long minute later, Jules and Adrianna joined her.

"That was professional acting, right there," said Jules. "You make a perfect pouty princess."

Corrie punched him lightly on the shoulder.

"I told you we'd figure out distractions on the spot."

JULES

Corrie was an artist, no doubt about it. The way she had twisted the pool worker around her little finger, and left him with no suspicions at all, was pure genius. If Jules hadn't been impressed with her before—and he was, no doubt about it—that would have sealed the deal.

"Now what, boss?" he said to Corrie. Her mouth twisted in thought.

"In through the bedroom, I guess. Check them first, like Adrianna suggested, then look in the main area. It's the most likely to have Miles in it, so we'll leave it until last."

"There's a balcony door around the corner." Adrianna pointed. "Let's use that."

Corrie led the charge at a half-crouch to avoid being seen from the windows. Jules hugged the wall as he watched. Corrie's encounter with the pool worker had nearly given him a heart attack, but the longer they went without seeing a person, the less his stomach felt like it was filled with electric eels.

Corrie peeked through a window. When she waved them forward, Jules took a deep breath and went first to the balcony door. It was unlocked. He wondered what they would have done if it hadn't been.

"Not much need for security on a private island, I guess," he whispered to the others. Corrie nodded.

"Lucky us."

Jules stepped onto plush, cream-colored carpeting. His shoes left bits of fir needles in the loops, for which he was not sorry in the least. Miles had taken his best friend. If he had to clean his carpets after their rescue effort, Jules wasn't going to cry about it.

There was a king-sized bed covered with a puffy white duvet, and a large mirror over a vanity. All the furniture was artfully carved from what looked like treefalls from the property. It was elegant and yet ostentatious, and Jules disliked it immensely while still coveting the luxury. It was a far cry from his little trailer with its worn sheets and chipping cabinet fronts.

The room was otherwise empty, and Adrianna walked to the door to open it. Jules looked in the closet to make sure Zeb wasn't tied up in there. When Adrianna gave a squeak of surprise, he grabbed Corrie's arm and shoved her in the empty closet. He followed and closed the door quietly behind them.

"What's going on?" Corrie whispered. Jules put a hand over her mouth. Her soft lips protested for a moment, but they stilled when Adrianna's voice spoke.

"Hi, there. Are you cleaning? I left my phone here the last time I visited."

"Here?" A middle-aged woman's voice spoke with suspicion. Adrianna laughed lightly.

"I know, how silly. I was snooping around at the work party. It's such a beautiful house, isn't it? Anyway, I was boating with my brother, and we stopped here to check for the phone. Miles had said it was all right when I texted him. No one answered my knock, though."

"Okay," the woman said, doubt still coloring her voice. "And you think it's here?"

"It's the last place I remember. Maybe by the night table?"

There was rummaging outside their closet door. Jules held his breath, his hand still over Corrie's mouth. She didn't move, and her breath was a warm breeze on his hand. Jules wondered what the plan was. Did Adrianna have an idea, or was she desperately figuring out her next move?

"There's nothing here," the woman said. Suspicion filled her voice. "We should find Mr. Callahan now. You shouldn't be walking around his house without him knowing."

"I don't want to disturb him," Adrianna said. "It must not be here. I'll go back to my boat."

"You should come with me," the woman said firmly. "Now."

There was the sound of footsteps.

"If you just listen," said Adrianna with desperation.

"Get out of my way," the woman said. "I'm getting Mr. Callahan right now. Out of my way!"

This had escalated too far. Jules took a deep breath then threw the closet door open and charged toward the woman, who wore an apron and sensible shoes, her graying hair tied up in a kerchief. He wrapped an arm around her torso and clamped a hand over her mouth.

"Jules!" Corrie whisper-screamed. "Now what?"

The woman grunted and struggled. Jules pulled her tighter.

"I'm open to suggestions," Jules gasped. "Anyone? She's stronger than she looks."

Adrianna pulled a syringe out of her pocket. With a look of determination, she took off the lid, primed the syringe, and stuck it in the woman's neck. Adrianna threw the syringe aside, and she and Corrie held the woman's legs tight against the ground while Jules fought with the woman's bucking torso. It felt like an hour before the woman stopped struggling but couldn't have been more than three minutes. Her weight pulled her to the ground, and Jules didn't resist. When she stopped moving, he and Corrie stared with open mouths at Adrianna.

"What?" Adrianna said. "Did you have a better idea?"

"Since when did you start carrying around sedatives in your pocket?" Corrie said faintly.

"Since we plotted a rescue mission." Adrianna grinned with mischief in her eyes. "I'm training to be a vet. Sometimes I have these things lying around. I'm only thankful that the dose worked on her. That syringe was meant for a cougar."

"Amazing," Jules said. He meant it. These women were smart, beautiful, and now fierce. He shook his head with admiration.

"Thanks for leaping to my defense," said Adrianna. "That

was quick thinking. Nice work."

"It was either that or have Molly Maid here raise the alarm." Jules was pleased with himself, but he didn't need to advertise the fact. One brave act did not a hero make. He was still Jules, creeping in the footsteps of daring women. He grabbed the maid by her ankles and dragged her to the other side of the bed, so she wouldn't be seen from the door.

Corrie looked in the hallway then waved them forward. It led to a doorway through which light poured.

"That must be the open area," Corrie breathed. "Ready?"

Jules would never be ready, but that didn't matter. Corrie poked her head out. No one must have been there, because she stepped into the light. Jules followed.

His first glance took in the view, which was beautiful if you didn't take frequent trips on the *Clicker*. That sort of forested-island scenery was the norm for Jules. His second glance saw the kitchen in the open-concept room, and his breath caught in his throat.

Forget the view. If he ever won the lottery, this would be the kitchen he would buy. Gleaming granite counters, a gas range with six burners, two ovens, a fridge big enough to hold three turkeys…

Adrianna's voice broke him out of his reverie.

"Do you think they're in the aquarium?"

ZEBALLOS

Zeb itched all over. His skin was on fire. He was desperate to sink into cool water, to feel soothing salt and tingling currents all over his body and let the water heal his discomfort.

How long were they going to let him rot here for? The basement was not a habitable one. It was uneven, blasted out of bedrock and only high enough to crouch in. Flint had grumbled darkly when he had pushed Zeb down here and tied his legs together again. Now Zeb lay in the musty dark on bare rock, his skin pressed against the jagged surface. The best thing he could say was that the stone was cool on his feverish skin.

It felt like an eternity before light blazed above him from the crawlspace's trapdoor but was probably only hours. Flint grunted above him.

"Come on, the boss thinks you've had enough time to think. I'm getting bored, so I'd be happier if you didn't speak right away, personally. Gives me something to do."

Flint cut the rope binding Zeb's legs together. He hauled Zeb toward the trapdoor so that Zeb could stand. He tried to do so, but it took a minute for his tingling legs to hold his weight.

"Are you sick or something?" Flint said with a look of disgust. "What's wrong with you? You're burning up."

Zeb shrugged and maintained a stoic silence. Flint didn't need to know what the problem was. If they knew what real torture was for him, he would never be allowed to touch saltwater again. It wasn't likely he'd get to immerse himself anytime soon, but he didn't want to pound the final nail in his proverbial coffin.

Flint shoved and prodded Zeb up the trapdoor and hauled himself up behind Zeb. Miles stood before them with a smug expression. Zeb longed to wipe it off.

"Is it my turn now, Mr. Callahan?" said Flint in a hopeful tone. Miles smiled indulgently.

"I have a better idea. Take him to the aquarium. I think our friend here would rather show, not tell."

Flint sighed with disappointment, but he pulled Zeb to his feet and pushed him ahead. Miles led the way out of the large closet, through a hallway to the main area. He walked to a wide set of double doors, made of frosted glass and sandblasted with depictions of sea lions and long strands of swirling kelp. Zeb hadn't been impressed with the house so far—he didn't care about big views and expensive furniture—but if he ever had money, those doors would be the first thing he would install in a home.

Miles pushed both doors open with a theatrical gesture. They swung open easily on well-oiled hinges. Zeb's eyes widened.

The large room beyond was dimly lit from the light of seven fish tanks. These were no typical home tanks—each was built-in, and half of them reached from floor to ceiling. The tanks along the walls housed exotic creatures. There were jellyfish of all types, squids, and strange fish that Zeb had only ever heard about.

The focal point, however, was the tank along the back wall. It curved outward into the room and spanned the entire space. Zeb had no idea the volume of water the tank held, but three of him could stretch out toe to head along the front. Inside swam five sharks.

Four of them looked familiar, at least from books. The last one confused Zeb at first. Was it a white-spotted bamboo shark? Then he saw the slits in the pectoral fins and knew. Miles had a kroll in his aquarium. Did he even know what he had?

"Do you like my aquarium?" Miles said with a satisfied smile. He waved at the tanks. "It's my pride and joy. I won't tell you how many tens of thousands of dollars I spent on collecting these rare specimens, but I feel it was worth it."

Zeb said nothing. He didn't want to give Miles the satisfaction of seeing any awe on his face. He glanced again at the kroll. Miles saw the direction of his gaze.

"Ah, yes, a new acquisition. I haven't yet had my expert identify it for me. Fascinating, isn't it? It must be very rare to not be in any books."

Zeb didn't hide his derision. Miles was an idiot. Krolls had a highly poisonous bite. If any of the other sharks got on its bad side, they were toast.

"You won't tell me what I want to know," said Miles. "So, you'll show me what I want to know. Flint, take him to the back. He can show us how fast he can swim away from the sharks. They haven't been fed yet, and they look hungry."

Flint grinned and gestured toward a narrow entry to his left. Zeb glanced at the shark tank again. He was supposed to be frightened, but his first thought was that he would have a swim. It felt like forever since his late-night dip that had ended so disastrously. It was too bad he didn't have any jellyfish to snack on.

He shook himself into reality. Hungry sharks were no laughing matter, and any use of his dexterity or strength underwater would confirm Miles' suspicions. And what if they thought he was on this enhancer, and then found out his abilities were natural? What would they do to him?

Zeb felt cold despite his fevered skin. This was what Krista was always warning him about. What used to feel like his sister's paranoia now seemed like sensible advice.

What were his options? Zeb looked around. Miles watched him, but Gavin checked his watch and Flint was fiddling with a switchblade. Maybe this was his chance.

Zeb dived to the side, out of reach of Flint's hands. He rolled and awkwardly scrambled upright without using his arms. The double doors were only steps away. If he could make it down the stairs and to the water's edge, he would be home free. It wasn't that far to swim to the *Clicker*, not for him.

A paralyzing cramping through every muscle in his body knocked him over and pinned him to the ground. His limbs shook helplessly. When the pain stopped, he gasped for air. Rough hands lifted him to his feet.

"Try that again," Flint growled. "And the sharks will snack on your arm as an appetizer."

Zeb felt drained after the taser attack. He hadn't passed out this time, but it was a close thing. Flint hit him again on his jaw, and a trickle of blood dribbled down his chin from a split lip. Flint pushed him, and he stumbled forward to the small passageway behind a panel near the door.

"Avoid bullets, please, Flint," Miles said behind them. "I don't want my tanks damaged. You're authorized for any other force you deem necessary. Did you hear that, Mr. Artino? I want you in that shark tank. You're going to stay there until you've shown me what I want to see."

Flint gave him another push. The passage was narrow and full of bubbling pipes on one side. Zeb squeezed past. He tried desperately to think of a way out of this, but his mind was wooly from the taser's effects, and it was enough effort to force one foot in front of the other.

"Hurry up," Flint said. "I can't wait for this gig to be done. You've been more hassle than you're worth. I just about died from boredom at the beginning, and now you're getting feisty. Don't get me wrong, I like a challenge, but the shark tank thing is too hands-off for my liking. I prefer to get personal."

There was a ladder on the wall. Flint prodded Zeb to start climbing. Zeb put one foot on the ladder, then another. He blinked the wooziness away. Could he kick Flint's face, make his escape somehow? He glanced down. Flint was carefully out of reach and watching him closely. When he saw Zeb looking, he grinned.

"I'm wise to your tricks. Just get in the tank. If the sharks maul you too much, I'll fish you out so we can give what's left of your body back to your family. Sound like a fair deal?"

Zeb turned back to the ladder. He might as well get in the water and have done with it. At least in the salty coolness, he would feel at home. Maybe it would help his mind recover so he could think of a plan. The sharks shouldn't be a problem.

Zeb tasted blood in his mouth and grimaced. If he didn't dip his head under and expose the sharks to the scent of his blood, it would be fine. He hoped.

"Hurry up," said Flint. "Mr. Callahan wants a show. I'll be waiting at the top of the ladder. No tricks."

Zeb's head rose above the tank's top. The water's surface moved with the bubbling of pumps and the sharks' swimming. Despite the circumstances, it looked inviting.

Zeb swung his legs over the side. When his feet hit the water, he let out a moan of longing. Before he could think too hard about it, he slid his body into the blissfully wet and cool water, careful to keep his head above the surface.

Too late, he noticed a stream of dilute red diffusing out from his neck. The blood must have dripped off his chin. He looked back at the ladder, but Flint was now perched at the top with a knife in one hand and a nasty smile on his face.

"No getting out here, I'm afraid. The only way out is in."

There was no point in keeping his head above the surface, not with his blood already in the water. He might as well submerge and deal with the sharks the best he could. The skin on his head ached from his denial of seawater, anyway. He took a deep breath and sunk below the surface.

Zeb's eyes adjusted to the water, and the ache in his head dissipated. Sharp sounds in the air subsided into the muffled pulse of water. There were clicks from encrusting coral on the wall, and a deep moan from a hidden plainfin midshipman. The sharks were silent, but Zeb had expected that. They had noticed his blood. They had been moving randomly throughout the tank, but now they swam in tight semicircles around him, one eye always staring at him. That wasn't good. He was a target.

He felt better underwater, but still not fully recovered from the taser hit. He could see nothing outside the reflective wall of glass. His world had constricted to this tank full of menacing sharks. His heartrate accelerated when a shark darted close to him before shying away. There was no way out of this, and he was panicking. When the next shark darted toward him, Zeb burst sideways in a flurry of movement to a far corner of the tank. He wedged himself between two fake rocks and tried to calm himself.

The sharks weren't large, but that didn't matter if there were five of them. One bite from the kroll would finish him, anyway. He had to win them over, convince him that he wasn't food worth eating. His mind flashed through the different sounds he had successfully used with wild sharks.

The five had repositioned themselves and resumed their patrol, tightening their circles with every pass. Zeb closed his eyes. He let forth a multitude of clicks, moans, and squeaks, mimicking a mother killer whale. The whales were ferocious predators, and these small sharks were no match for one, especially since the whales hunted in pods. He wouldn't pass for a full-size killer whale, but maybe he could look like a strange calf. Hopefully, they would become disoriented by the potential threat and ignore him.

With a start, four of the sharks darted away to a far corner of the tank, where they circled warily. The kroll, however, approached him with curiosity. Zeb clenched his jaw. Did the kroll even know what a killer whale was, wherever it usually lived? How could he scare it away?

The kroll swam back and forth in front of Zeb, close enough to touch. If Zeb had been normal, he would have hyperventilated long ago. As it was, he hardly moved, for fear that the kroll would attack with those poisonous teeth. Zeb didn't want to die, not today. What could he do?

What noise did the sonar device make? He'd seen a kroll attracted to it, but with no bloodlust. Maybe Zeb could recreate that frequency. Maybe it would calm the kroll. It was the only thing left to try.

Zeb hummed. He started low, then went lower. It wasn't

quite right, and the kroll circled closer. He sent the sound deep in his throat and chest, deeper than he'd ever attempted before. The kroll stared at him, ever moving.

That was it. Zeb recognized the frequency from the sonar device, except it was coming from his own chest. He kept making the noise while he watched the kroll. How would it react?

When Zeb reached the correct frequency, the kroll paused as if listening. Then it swam directly at Zeb. He didn't even have time to stop his sound before the kroll brushed against his arm and then swam past. It had rough skin like sandpaper that grated Zeb's skin painfully, but he wasn't bitten. The kroll came back for another pass and grazed Zeb's stomach, leaving a red welt but nothing else.

It was rubbing against him like a cat. Zeb stared at it, soaking in every detail and committing it to memory. The kroll's eyes had a vertical, oval-shaped pupil surrounded by a mottled blue and green iris which mesmerized Zeb. He'd forgotten that detail from his mother's stories, or perhaps she hadn't mentioned it.

Zeb stopped making the sound, ready to start again if needed, but the kroll lost interest as soon as he grew quiet. It swam off to examine another part of the tank.

Zeb slumped over in relief. He'd made it. He'd successfully waylaid four hungry sharks and a kroll, and he was still alive. He wondered what Miles was thinking right now and glanced at the mirrored surface of the glass. Belatedly, he remembered that a normal person would have surfaced ages ago to breathe. How long had he been down here? He certainly didn't need air yet, so it must have been less than ten minutes. He kicked quickly to the surface to gulp a breath of air for show.

"I wondered if you'd died down there," Flint said. "I thought about finding a net to haul you up, but that seemed like a lot of work."

There was a loud bang and some shouts. Flint frowned.

"What the hell are they doing out there?" he said. When Zeb moved as if to climb out, Flint brandished the knife at him. "Don't even think about it. You're staying in the tank until Mr. Callahan says otherwise."

Zeb glared at Flint with frustration. What was going on out there? He needed to know. With another gulp of air, he dived into the tank once more.

He swam directly to the glass. It wasn't made to be reflective—that was only how the refraction of light through water made it appear. Could he see out if he were closer? He pressed his face to the glass and looked.

Everything was blurry, but there were three figures, not two. The new figure was a small woman with dark-brown hair in a ponytail. His heart squeezed with fear.

What was Corrie doing here?

CORRIE

Corrie heard voices coming from the open door of the aquarium. She paused and peeked her head around the frame. The others were right behind her. Her heartbeat was an irregular staccato, but she had to know what was going on.

Her eyes were immediately drawn to the large shark tank along the back wall. She froze. Zeb was in the tank, underwater with his eyes open, his red swimsuit bright and his normally tanned skin pale under the aquarium lights. Although four sharks huddled in the far corner of the tank, the strange spotted shark circled in front of him, clearly interested in the captive Zeb.

The spotted shark darted at him, and Corrie almost let out a squeak of fear. What was Miles doing to him? Why was he in the tank? Zeb held himself stiffly between two rocks, his gaze trained on the shark as it swam.

Zeb's eyes narrowed in concentration. What was he doing? It was something, because the spotted shark paused its ceaseless movements. Then, it swam straight for Zeb.

Before Corrie could react, the shark rubbed against Zeb and came back for another pass. Corrie's heart was in her mouth, but she frowned. The spotted shark wasn't attacking. It was… nuzzling? Zeb grimaced at the motion but held still.

The shark must have grown tired of the game, for it swam away to circle the other sharks instead. Zeb kicked his legs to reach the surface, and Corrie realized how long he had been under the water for. His free diving must have really increased his lung capacity.

Corrie felt a breeze behind her. She turned. Jules and Adrianna were sneaking through a half-open door to their right that led into a small corridor lined with pipes. She took a step to follow them—they were clearly trying to get Zeb out of the tank—but paused when she heard talking.

"Well, that didn't work." The smooth voice of Miles Callahan emerged from the dimness to the right of the tank. "I expected a few bites, at least. I wanted him to talk after this, soften him up, you know?"

"Let my colleague Flint soften him up for you,' said the other man in a precise voice. "It is his specialty."

"I suppose so." Miles waved at the tank. "Better get him out for more questions. Did you see him swim, though? That was faster than normal. Way faster. I'm sure he's on the enhancer. I tell you, Gavin, this is the next big thing. We have to get this guy to talk."

"We will," said Gavin in reassurance, but Corrie had heard enough.

"Miles!" she cried, rushing forward. "Get him out of there! What are you doing?"

Miles turned. His face registered confusion.

"Corrie?" It took a moment for him to shake off his bewilderment and turn on his charm, but it came out soon enough. "How did you get here? Never mind, it's lovely to see you. Are you speaking of him?" Miles waved at Zeb in the tank, who dived under the water once more. "Not to worry. He's a fully trained shark biologist. He's examining my sharks for me, making sure they are healthy, and the tank is functioning properly. I take care of my assets."

"Liar," Corrie said with venom. Miles looked shocked that someone would dare to speak to him like that. Corrie felt that it was past time someone did. "He's my friend, and you kidnapped him."

Zeb was now pressed against the glass of the tank. He looked frightened again, but this time, not for himself. He waved at Corrie to leave. The sharks were circling again, and they looked agitated.

"This man is your friend," Miles said slowly. "Then—do you know about the enhancer?"

Corrie said nothing, but her expression must have given her

away, because Miles smiled.

"Well, this is a turn of events that I hadn't anticipated. How many know of it? You are a marvel, knowing about the enhancer and keeping quiet about it. I can only assume you haven't thought through the implications of what such a discovery means to the world. To be able to increase strength and speed underwater, what a feat! There are endless applications. And what if we could transfer the technology to above water? What could humanity achieve?"

"You just want to sell it, to the military or some big company," Corrie spat out. "You want the money, and the reputation as cutting-edge. You don't care about the implications, either."

"You harangue these 'big companies,' Corrie, but think of what could actually happen. What if this technology was the basis for curing diseases? We have no idea of the uses of this enhancer, or what it can be made to do. Maybe it could help us figure out how to cure childhood diabetes. Who knows? What is it doing on the cellular level? Maybe it could be used to combat aggressive cancers by enhancing surrounding cells. You're a scientist. Surely, you can see the potential for good here."

Corrie stared at him. On some level, he was right. Great discoveries had been made from natural products, studied and reproduced and modified in the lab. Her own work aimed to look at cancer-fighting compounds in bacteria that dwell in anemones. Who knew what the unicorn fish slime could do, given enough research and testing?

Miles pressed his point, clearly sensing her indecision.

"You already know something. You are perfectly positioned to take the lead on this research. This is an opportunity to make a difference, do something huge and good in the world. You could be the lead scientist on this research, your name on all the papers, your direction and vision guiding the team. This is big, Corrie. Do you want to be a part of it?"

Corrie allowed herself a moment to imagine the picture that Miles painted. She couldn't deny the draw it had on her. She wanted to make a splash, to do science that really mattered, to make a difference in the world. He was right—this discovery had that potential. And Miles didn't know the half of it. There were far more fish in the sea than he knew. What other important compounds did they produce that could be used for the greater good?

But there was the rub. No matter how much Corrie wanted the end goal, there was no justification for Miles' methods. If she brought the unicorn fish and its properties to the world's attention, it would be on her terms, and on good terms.

"You're trying to convince me that the end justifies the means. It doesn't work that way. You can't go beating up Matt and dropping Zeb in a shark tank just to get answers. You'll do anything to get what you want, and I can't be a part of that."

"It's an important role, ushering in the future." Miles gave her a sleek smile, but Corrie could sense the sourness behind it. "Staying on top of things is not a job for the slow or meek."

"You can do it the right way, or the wrong way," Corrie said. She couldn't believe she had ever fallen to this man's charms. He was cold and calculating with no understanding of how humans should behave. She thought of Zeb suddenly. He might have secrets, but he'd never yet given her reason to distrust his motives. She glanced at the tank, and her stomach dropped. Five sharks swam lazily in the water, alone. Where was Zeb?

Miles shrugged.

"I gave you a chance to be a part of this. But if you're not on board, we'll have to do this the hard way. Gavin?"

Corrie's eyes peeled away from the Zeb-free tank and focused on the approaching Gavin. His expression was disinterested, which was more terrifying than if he had been leering savagely. Corrie had the impression that he could do anything without changing his bland bank teller mien.

Corrie backed away until her shoulders were against the wall next to the half-open door that lead to the pipe-filled corridor. Gavin pulled a knife out from his belt.

"We'll have to do this the old-fashioned way, I'm afraid," he said calmly. "I would threaten you with a gun, but Mr. Callahan doesn't want to risk his aquarium. Now, be a good girl and tell Mr. Callahan all about the fish with the horn."

Corrie barely breathed. Her mind flitted to the improbability of her scientific career leading to being held at knifepoint by the henchman of a rich opportunist over the secrets of a legendary fish. What could she do now? None of her undergrad courses had prepared her for this.

"Let her go."

Adrianna's voice sounded sweeter than honey to Corrie's terrified ears. She didn't know what Adrianna could do, but having her here was infinitely better than being alone.

Corrie turned her head to look at her friend. Adrianna held a gasping bundle in her arms. A long tail flopped nearly to her knees, and a vicious-looking head opened and closed its toothy mouth sporadically. It was the spotted shark that had rubbed against Zeb.

"This shark has a poisonous bite," Adrianna said clearly. "Let Corrie go, or I will let it bite you."

Gavin huffed through his nose. It was a small noise of derision, the closest Corrie had seen of emotion from the goon.

"We'll deal with you in a minute," he said.

"Get the fish, Gavin," Miles said sharply. "It needs to be in the water. I paid good money for that shark. I don't want my investment wasted."

Without warning, Gavin lunged at the shark with his arms outstretched to take the bundle from Adrianna. Adrianna screamed and pointed the snout of the shark at Gavin. The shark opened its mouth wide.

Sharp teeth sliced Gavin's arm, shearing cleanly through his suit jacket. Blood splattered on the floor. Gavin stumbled backward, clutching his injured arm to his chest. His face contorted with pain.

Corrie didn't wait for a second opportunity. Jules and Zeb were right behind Adrianna. She pointed them all to the door of the aquarium and they moved as one. Miles shouted behind them, but Corrie didn't look back. They had Zeb—that was all that mattered.

ZEBALLOS

One moment, Zeb had been watching Corrie confront Miles through the glass and be threatened by Gavin, helpless to stop them from hurting her. The next moment, a sharp rapping on the tank wall caught his attention and he surfaced.

"Jules?" he gasped when he saw who it was. "Where's the goon?"

"Sedated on the ground," Jules said with a grin. "Adrianna has skills. Come on. We have to get out of here."

Zeb swam to the edge but paused before getting out. He couldn't leave the kroll in here. Miles would eventually find out what it was—or what it wasn't. He couldn't leave a creature from his mother's world in the clutches of that man. He dunked his head underwater and repeated the hum that had attracted the kroll before.

It swam up to him without hesitation. He carefully grasped it around the middle, and it stayed calm in his arms. His head surfaced.

"Jules," he gasped. "Give me your sweater."

To his credit, Jules didn't question his request. Zeb took the sweater and wrapped it around the shark, then lifted the whole bundle above the water. The kroll flipped its tail feebly a few times, but Zeb's calming noise from before must have told it that it was in good hands, and it didn't struggle.

On the ground, Adrianna stood beside Flint's prone body. His head was bleeding from a gash on his temple, and his mouth hung slackly open.

"What are you doing with that shark?" she gasped.

"It doesn't belong here," Zeb said firmly. "We're taking it."

He took a step forward and stumbled. His legs, now that he was on land, felt feeble and wobbly.

"What the hell did they do to you?" Jules muttered. "Adrianna, can you take the fish? I'll help Zeb."

Adrianna reached out for the kroll.

"Don't touch the teeth," Zeb said. "Very poisonous. I think it will stay calm for now, but we need to hurry. It can't breathe."

Adrianna didn't waste any time. She ran ahead, and by the time Zeb and Jules made their awkward way to the door, Corrie pointed them forward and took off at a run.

Zeb could hardly keep up. Corrie darted ahead with nimble footsteps. Adrianna was close behind, despite her heavy load of wriggling, suffocating kroll. Jules still held his arm for support, but it was more of a hindrance than a help at this speed.

"I'm fine," Zeb gasped. "Just run."

Jules gave him an unsure glance, but there was no time to argue. Shouting drifted from behind them. Miles and the goons must be on their heels. Zeb gritted his teeth and concentrated on moving his sluggish legs. He hoped it wasn't far to wherever they were going. He didn't have much stamina left after his incarceration and the taser attacks, not to mention the throbbing ache in his jaw. He felt a trickle of blood oozing down his chin from the wound that hadn't yet had a chance to clot.

The shouting was getting closer, but the trees parted to reveal a stony beach and open sky. Zeb had never been so glad to see the ocean, and that was saying a lot.

Corrie slipped her way to a small dock where the *Clicker*'s dinghy was tied up. Jules followed, but Adrianna paused by the water's edge. The kroll flopped feebly. Its gills were probably almost dry by now, and Zeb felt a pang of sympathy. He knew what it was like to need the water.

"Give it to me," he said to Adrianna. He wrapped his arms around the kroll, and Adrianna released her hold.

"Put it back quick," she said with a glance to the forest. "They're coming."

She took off at a run toward the nearby dock. Zeb splashed

into the surf, the water cool and welcoming against his thighs. The kroll was nearly motionless now. Even its gills only fluttered intermittently. Zeb knelt and laid the fish in the water. When he rolled it out of Jules' sweater, the kroll didn't move.

"Come on," Zeb said, frustration making his voice sharp. "Start swimming!"

He pushed the fish forward to force water through its gills.

Its tail wiggled. Then, with a weak shake, the fish twisted out of Zeb's grasp and disappeared into the green water. Zeb sagged with relief, waves splashing over his torso.

"Get back here!"

Miles' angry voice sent a spike of adrenaline through Zeb's system. Fear sweat washed into the splashing water. He looked around. Miles was on the stony beach, waving a taser in the air and looking furious.

Corrie and the others stood on the dock, waving and shouting at him frantically. It was closer to swim to them than to get back on the beach. Zeb set out with sure strokes, his aches and weak legs stronger in the water. Miles ran parallel to the beach toward the dock, gesticulating wildly.

Zeb was almost at the dock when he felt it. A wave of pressure hit him, as if something large passed by him in the water. He tuned in with his other senses and received only an impression of great length. His senses were always thrown off by surf, so he ignored the feeling and pulled himself onto the dock. Miles was already at the far end.

Jules was in the dinghy, pulling at the motor's cord. Corrie untied the painter.

"Get in!" she yelled. "Hurry!"

Adrianna leaped into the little vessel, then everything shook. Zeb fell to his hands and knees. What had happened? Was it an earthquake?

Another tremendous crash shook the dock. Miles stopped, wariness replacing the anger in his features. Zeb met Corrie's eyes from her position on hands and knees. She looked as wide-eyed and confused as himself.

Then, a tail whipped out of the water. It was massive and a murky dark green. It tapered to a fine point, which Zeb only had a moment to appreciate before it fell with an earth-shattering crash onto the dock. The wood was no match for such a force, and the planks splintered into thousands of pieces. Zeb covered his face to avoid flying debris.

"What the hell was that?" Miles shouted from across the void. "Get back here and give me some answers!"

The tail emerged again and crashed onto the dock, closer to Miles. He shrieked and fell backward. Zeb stood. He knew what it was. This was the ligan. His mother had told him how loyal ligans were. The one he'd befriended must have followed the boat then felt his distress and come to protect him.

While he was intensely grateful for the ligan's interference, Zeb knew he needed to stop it before it got out of hand. As much as he hated Miles and his machinations, Zeb wasn't quite ready to murder him for it. Even if the ligan did the deed, Zeb would always know he could have stopped it.

Zeb took a step forward and pretended to trip. The last thing he heard before he plunged headfirst into the water, in the most graceless entry he'd ever accomplished, was Corrie's sharp scream.

In the water, Zeb concentrated and hummed the frequency of the sonar device. It had worked on the kroll. Hopefully the ligan would respond as well.

Zeb felt the ligan approach before he saw it. A moment later, the massive head of the ligan emerged through the murk next to Zeb's face. Zeb stopped the hum and made a few clicks and hums of appreciation. He had no idea if the ligan would understand, but he had no other recourse. He reached out a hand to the cheek of the ligan. The gigantic beast allowed him to touch the scaly surface. Then, with a rolling, sinuous motion, the ligan turned and slid away from the island.

Zeb closed his eyes with momentary relief. Then, he recalled

Corrie's agonized scream when he had "fallen" into the sea. He'd already caused enough anguish to his friends. It was time to join them.

He popped his head out of the water. Corrie was on her knees, searching the waves. Adrianna had her hand to her mouth with a look of horror, and Jules was pale.

"I'm fine," he said as he pulled himself to the dock. "It's gone."

Corrie shook her head at him in bewilderment and gave him a sharp look.

"You know that for sure?" she asked. He nodded, and she said, "Okay."

Zeb had a feeling that this was the start of a longer conversation that was currently paused while they dealt with the situation at hand. He would be in for a reckoning later, he was sure. For some reason, the thought didn't terrify him as much as it had used to.

CORRIE

Corrie turned to Miles, who was gingerly working his way to the edge of the broken dock.

"Stop right there," she said. "And listen."

Miles looked at Corrie in astonishment.

"What could you possibly say to me?" he sneered. "You know, even if you get away now, I will find him. I have resources. And if you tell anyone about this little debacle, no one will believe you. I'm a respected member—and donor—of the community, and you are nobody. Again, I have resources."

"Wow," said Corrie. "Just—wow. You know what? You're right. You could probably worm your way out of any accusation we throw at you. Sad, but true." She dug her hand into her pocket and pulled out her phone. "But you know what you can't deny? Evidence." She started reading from the list Krista had sent her. "Fifty thousand dollars from the Hagan foundation to your private account. That was a tidy profit at the expense of those people awaiting treatment. A silencing payout to Courtney Gauthier, who then wrote a confession— she, the money, and the confession all disappeared. Another signed confession from Henry Stilwell, detailing the shadowy side of a hostile takeover."

Miles' face drained of blood with every word Corrie spoke. She felt a grim satisfaction but tried to keep her expression stern.

"I can silence you, you know," he said finally.

Corrie grew cold at the thought but didn't let it show.

"You could," she said calmly. "But if we don't come home, the person who sent me these documents will know what you did. And, trust me, she will take you down."

Miles tried to keep his face smooth, but he was unsuccessful at hiding his panic.

"What do you want?" he said finally.

"What do you think?" Corrie said. "Stop hunting Zeb. Stop looking for the enhancer. Stop trying to find weird fish. Leave all that alone. Stop being such a shady bastard, while you're at it. If you don't, or if you try to hurt us, or if we catch wind of anything less than upstanding, those documents are getting out. Got it?"

Miles' jaw worked.

"I'm sorry, I can't hear you," Corrie said loudly. "Do we have an agreement?"

"We have an agreement," Miles said stiffly over the crashing waves.

"Right, that's settled." Corrie made a shooing motion with her hands. "Off you go. I hope your goon recovers from the poison, but I won't hold my breath."

Miles looked murderous, but he turned and strode up the beach without looking back. When he finally disappeared into the woods, Corrie turned to Zeb and threw her arms around him.

"I'm so glad you're okay," she said into his neck. His arms tightened around her. She wondered how terrified he must have been, trapped and hopeless. She tried not to notice his smooth, wet muscles under her hands. She released him. "Did they hurt you a lot?"

"Nothing I can't recover from," he said then winced and rubbed his jaw gingerly. "A bit beat up."

Corrie wiped a trickle of blood from a cut on his lip with her sleeve. His eyes followed her hand, and she dropped it to her side.

"Come on," she said to break the moment. "Let's get you back to the *Clicker*. It's not far."

Zeb's shoulders slumped in relief.

"I don't think I've ever heard more appealing words than that."

Jules gave Zeb a brief hug in the dinghy, then slapped his

friend's back and put the motor into drive. No one said much on the way to the boat. Corrie and Adrianna huddled together, Adrianna looking as overwhelmed as Corrie felt. At the *Clicker*, Jules climbed aboard and got the winch prepared for the dinghy. Once everyone was on deck, Corrie held up her hand.

"No one else is bringing it up, so I will," she said. "What the hell was that tail? Anyone have a notion?"

Adrianna shrugged. Zeb and Jules glanced at each other.

"I'm not sure," said Zeb. "There are more mysteries out there, I guess."

Corrie stared hard at Zeb, but he avoided her gaze. He knew something—he always knew something—but he wouldn't tell her. This had to stop. Either she was in this with him or she wasn't.

She didn't say anything else, but she resolved to bring it up later when she was alone with Zeb. Zeb disappeared into the cabin to change, and Jules went to haul anchor. Adrianna turned to Corrie.

"That was insane." Adrianna leaned against the railing and sighed. "We made it. I'm going to sleep for a week after that adrenaline rush."

"I'm with you there." Corrie joined her friend on the railing, and they gazed at the waves rolling by.

"I can't believe you didn't say how fit Zeb is," Adrianna said in a conversational tone. Corrie coughed in surprise.

"What?"

"You got a whole week of him wandering around in that speedo?" Adrianna nudged Corrie. "No wonder you want to go out for another week. Maybe I should start researching anemones. I didn't realize the scenery was so pleasant."

"Stop it," said Corrie with an embarrassed laugh. "I'm dating David, remember?"

"Who said anything about dating? I've been with Patrick for over a year—a very happy year, mind you—but it doesn't mean I don't have eyes and a pulse."

Corrie elbowed Adrianna.

"You're terrible."

"I'm just saying, if you enjoy embracing nearly naked men on these cruises of yours, I don't blame you." Adrianna winked. Corrie gave a melodramatic sigh.

"You're incorrigible. Come on, let's see what there is to eat. I'm starving."

ZEBALLOS

Zeb looked in the tiny mirror in his cabin. The side of his face was swelling and turning purple already. The blood had stopped flowing, finally, but he looked a mess. He opened a bottle of pills and swallowed two, hoping they would do something to dull the ache. He wanted to lie down on his bunk and not move until tomorrow, but he opened his cabin door instead. The others needed to see that he was okay, and that their rescue mission was a success. Jules, especially, wouldn't believe he was all right unless he was acting like normal. Zeb could pretend for him.

He climbed up the narrow stairs. He avoided the galley, from which female voices emerged. He wasn't quite ready to face Corrie again. He knew that the hour of reckoning approached, and he wasn't sure how much to tell her. A part of him wanted to tell her everything and spill all his secrets, but the part that had kept him quiet for so many years balked at that notion. She did need to know more, though. She knew that he knew about the ligan, he could tell. She wouldn't let that slide.

Zeb ducked into the wheelhouse with a wince at the motion. Jules glanced at him.

"Hey, what are you doing here?" Jules looked critically at Zeb's face. "You look like an overripe eggplant."

"Thanks. Just what I wanted to hear." Zeb sat in the folding chair with a sigh. "Thanks for coming to get me."

"Yeah. I'm pretty great." Jules said. "I don't mind hearing it."

Zeb smiled then regretted it as his cheek erupted in shooting pains. He grimaced and put a hand to the offending spot.

"Do you want some ice?" Jules looked at him with concern. Zeb waved him off.

"In a bit. I'll drive, if you like. I'm starving."

"Got it," said Jules. Zeb could tell he was relieved to have something useful to do. "Something soft, by the look of it. Something I would serve my grandma."

"The one with the dentures?" Zeb said. Jules laughed.

"Exactly."

When Jules disappeared into the galley, Zeb took the captain's chair with a sigh and pulled out his phone. Krista answered on the first ring.

"Hello?"

"Hey, it's me," Zeb said through his swelling cheek. There was a long pause on the line.

"You idiot," Krista said finally, her voice thick. Zeb realized with surprise that she was crying. "You scared me half to death. I told you to watch your back. How could you be so stupid as to get caught?"

"I love you too," he said. "Everyone's fine."

"Why do you sound weird?"

"Sore jaw."

"Did they beat you up?" Krista hissed. Zeb could practically hear her swelling with indignation. "Slimy bastard. I hate him with every fiber of my being. I only wish I could have been there to punch him in his smarmy, rich, privileged face." She sighed explosively. "I guess the threat of litigation is the next best thing."

"That was great, by the way," Zeb said. "We escaped, then Miles came after us, then a ligan crashed the dock—I managed to stop it—but Miles was still coming after us. It was only Corrie telling him about those documents you found and threatening him with them that made him back off and promise not to follow us anymore."

"A ligan?" Krista sounded disbelieving. "You mean, one of those giant sea serpents?"

"Yeah. It was cool. We're friends."

"You're friends." Krista was silent for a moment. "You're so weird, you know that?"

"Yeah."

Krista sighed.

"So, was it rough? Did they hurt you a lot?"

"Honestly?" Zeb said, thinking it over. "The worst part wasn't the pain or being tied up and left in that dank basement for hours. The worst was the fear that I wouldn't be able to get in the water anytime soon. Like, I was legitimately terrified about what would happen if I didn't. I got so hot, and I felt terrible." He swallowed when he remembered the crawling sensation on his skin and the naked fear of not being in control of when he swam. "I don't know what's going on with me. It's never been like this before. Remember we went camping in the Okanagan once, when we were kids? I didn't swim for a whole week, and I was fine. It's only recently that it's been so crazy."

"Have you had any more fainting spells?"

Zeb was taken aback. What did that have to do with anything?

"No. Why?"

"I'm just making sure you're feeling okay, otherwise," Krista said quickly. "Look, I don't know what's going on with the swimming. We'll figure it out, okay? I'll buy you some jellyfish this afternoon and you can pick it up next time you visit. We'll get through it. I'm just glad you're okay."

There was a rustling at the door, and Corrie entered. She started to back out again when she saw that Zeb was on the phone, but he waved her in.

"I have to go. I'll talk to you soon, okay?"

"Stay safe, weirdo," she said with a catch in her voice.

Zeb put his phone in his pocket. Corrie held out her hand, which contained a bag of frozen peas in a tea towel.

"We thought you might need this," she said. "You're starting to swell pretty badly."

"Thanks," Zeb said. He pressed the bag carefully against his left cheek. It felt good, and he closed his eyes for a moment to enjoy the sensation.

"Jules asked me to give you this, too," Corrie said. She

placed a bowl on the dash. In it was a spoon and a small amount of what looked like mashed turnip. She eyed it doubtfully. "I'm not sure what it is. Jules said it was an old coastal remedy for jaw aches."

Zeb frowned and took a spoonful, then his face cleared. Jules had finely chopped dried jellyfish and added water to make a thick paste. Zeb shivered with relief as the flavor rolled over his tongue, and he resisted the urge to shovel it in his mouth as fast as he could. He took another slow bite despite his body screaming for more.

"Thanks. I'll take anything to get rid of the ache," he said. He put the spoon down, even though he wanted to lick the bowl until every morsel was gone. He needed to say things to Corrie, and they couldn't wait. "Thank you for coming to the island. You and the others took a big risk for me."

"Of course." Corrie put her hand on his arm that stretched to the wheel. It was a comforting, warm weight. "How could I do anything else?"

"You could have called the police, like a normal person," he said. His throbbing jaw couldn't manage a smile to accompany his joke, so he was grateful when Corrie laughed.

"Yeah, but then you would have been stuck in a shark tank for days. Who knows when they would have found you? And we knew exactly where you were. No, it was the only way. You were very calm and collected in that tank. I would have freaked out, plonked in the middle of those sharks." She shivered.

"I swim a lot," Zeb said quickly. "It was okay. Did you see the shark I took out of the tank?" They had been in such a rush, he didn't know if she had even noticed Adrianna carrying the kroll. Corrie's eyes grew wide.

"Yeah, I did. What was it? I didn't recognize it. Was it…"
She looked at Zeb expectantly. He nodded.
"I've never seen anything like it," he said truthfully.
"I wish I could have taken a sample," she said. "I feel like I

keep coming across these amazing opportunities and then squandering them."

"You got samples from the unicorn fish."

"Yeah, but Sucker, and that shark. And whatever was happening with that enormous tail." Corrie made a noise of frustration. "I'm greedy, I guess. I want more."

"What are you going to tell your professor?" What Zeb would say next depended greatly on what Corrie replied to this question. Corrie looked thoughtful.

"What on earth would I tell him? That there's been an evolutionary explosion and I'm on the forefront of discovery? I have evidence, but there is something bigger going on here. I want to know exactly what it is, before I even think about going to him with it. I don't understand what's happening, and that bothers me. I need a full story before I can decide on the version to tell others, what to hide and what to share, if anything. You know?"

Zeb nodded slowly. It was time.

"I want to show you something." Zeb pointed at the logbook he and Jules had been working on. It was tucked under a pile of charts on the counter. Corrie gave him a searching glance but reached for the book and flipped it open.

It was time to come clean, about some things, at least. Zeb hoped her enthusiasm for what she was about to see would outweigh her anger at his secret-keeping.

"I wasn't straight with you about the sonar device," he said in a rush. "It attracts strange creatures. I don't know how, or why. I've seen schools of strolias, a few krolls, even the ligan, since Jules and I figured out how the device works."

"Strolias?" Corrie said softly. She flipped a page and looked at Jules' sketch of one.

"Unicorn fish. Jules drew the pictures. The names are from stories my mother used to tell me. She knew all about these creatures. I don't know how, or why. That's why I'm out here, searching. I want to know more about her, and the creatures, and why she knew."

Zeb breathed heavily and turned to stare out the window in the direction they were headed. There was so much he couldn't say, but it felt good to tell Corrie some things, as if his secrets had been a weight around his neck until now. A ferry chugged along the horizon. Corrie flipped to another page.

"That tail that crashed into the dock, that was a ligan," she said quietly. "Wasn't it?"

"Yes."

Another page flipped.

"And your mother told you about these. Were there more?"

"Yes."

Zeb felt Corrie's excitement rachet up, as though it were a tangible thing. Then she closed the book with a snap.

"Why didn't you tell me before?" she asked in a calm voice, although her hurt was apparent. "I thought we were in this together."

There was nothing in the boat's path for a long distance, so Zeb turned to face Corrie. Her brown eyes gazed into his, looking for answers. He frowned.

"I know. I'm sorry. I was—" He swallowed. "I was afraid. Afraid you would tell your professor, that you would take it public. I'm not ready to do that. I want answers, not a prize for discovering a new species. I want to know what my mother knew and why, and that job will be more difficult if scientists and journalists and sport fishermen are crawling these waters, looking for new, crazy fish. I thought if I didn't tell you about the sonar device, you would be contained to your strolia sample."

Corrie was silent for a long while. Zeb started to sweat. He hoped he hadn't ruined everything with his omission, but he wouldn't blame her if he had. She looked into his eyes with puzzlement.

"So, why did you tell me now?" she asked.

"If I can't trust you after you risked your life to save me from

Miles, when can I?"

It took a while, but Corrie's face lifted in a sweet smile. Zeb breathed again. She took his hand in her delicate fingers and squeezed the palm.

"You can trust me," she said. "Let's do this together, okay? I won't tell my supervisor until you're comfortable with that. And I'll help you find answers, as long as you keep me in the loop."

"Deal," he said. When she let go of his hand, his felt strange without her warmth.

JULES

To say that Jules was relieved at the outcome of their adventure was an understatement. He almost kissed the deck of the *Clicker* when they boarded. He wasn't built for that kind of excitement. He was glad Zeb was okay and seemed his usual stoic self, although Jules could see that he was in pain. Jules didn't know why he didn't go straight to bed—he would have, in Zeb's shoes—but it was good to have him on board again, so Jules didn't push him away. Besides, he had a celebratory dinner to cook.

He put Corrie and Adrianna to work in the galley, despite the tight quarters. Adrianna tried her best to squeeze into the counter while she cut carrots. Corrie stayed in the dining area and set the table.

"There's no way I'm fitting in there, too," she said with a laugh. "I'll cheer you on from here."

"I forgot to say, earlier," said Adrianna. "Jules, you were amazing today. The way you charged out of the closet and tackled that cleaning woman, well, you really saved my bacon. The poor woman never knew what hit her."

A warm glow spread through Jules' chest, although he laughed off Adrianna's comment.

"You did the heavy lifting with that sedative. I'm glad you packed well for our rescue mission."

"No, Adrianna's right," Corrie said. "You just went for it. I was still frozen in the closet. Nicely done."

"Yeah, I had no idea what to do next," said Adrianna. "She was going to out me, for sure."

For once, Jules had the feeling that he wasn't a dead weight. Had he made a difference in their mission? It was a first. He quite liked the feeling. Maybe he wasn't always useless, given a chance. Mostly, but not always.

He couldn't say that he had enjoyed the mission, though. It

was way too stressful for him. Too many variables to go wrong, and the stakes were too high. He preferred vegetables. If they were overcooked—not that he would commit that blasphemy—it didn't truly matter.

Adrianna glanced at the stove, where four saucepans were bubbling away.

"How do you even know what's going on?" she asked. "Way too many pots on the go. And what if we hit a wave?"

"It's such a calm day, it's worth the risk. Zeb is pretty good at warning me when we're going to hit a rough patch. I can hold onto the handles until the waves pass."

"You like to live on the edge," Corrie said.

Jules shrugged. It was only cooking. What was a bit of sauce on the floor?

By the time dinner was ready, Zeb had pulled the *Clicker* into the marina and hooked the lines to cleats on the dock. The four of them squeezed onto the tiny bench around the table and Jules dished out spaghetti with meatballs.

"Jules, this is amazing," said Adrianna. "Seriously."

"I told you," said Corrie. "I got to eat this all week. I gained weight, I swear."

"It's only spaghetti," said Jules. "I thought we could use some comfort food."

"But the meatballs are so juicy, and you've put some kind of spice in the sauce that's different but so delicious," said Adrianna. She swallowed with a look of relish. "Have you considered going to culinary school, being a chef for a living? You'd go far."

Jules laughed and helped himself to more.

"Sounds like work," he said. "I don't mind what I'm doing."

The conversation changed course, but Jules turned Adrianna's words over in his mind. Culinary school—he'd never considered it. Hell, he'd never really thought that chefs went to school. And "chef" was such a hoity-toity word. He wasn't chef material. That was for snooty people in French restaurants who served caviar and raw steak.

What did they teach you in culinary school? He would have to look that up. Not that he was interested—he'd meant what he said, he liked his life as it was and didn't feel the need to do anything else—but he was curious, that was all. He'd never given it a thought before. There was nothing wrong with looking it up on the Internet.

CORRIE

Adrianna sped up to merge onto the highway on their way home from the *Clicker*.

"That was an insane day," she said.

"I didn't expect it when I woke up this morning," Corrie agreed. "Hop on a boat, drive to a private island, break out someone who was abducted—"

"Attack a man with a poisonous fish—"

"And dodge a giant sea serpent," Corrie finished. "Who is apparently friendly. To Zeb."

"You have interesting new friends," said Adrianna.

"Damn it," Corrie said. She wriggled out of the sweater Zeb had lent her when he had noticed her shivering. "I forgot to give Zeb back his sweater. I think they're leaving in the morning. Can you turn around?"

"It's not like he seems to get cold," Adrianna said, but she turned at the next exit and navigated her way back onto the highway in the opposite direction. "But, yeah, it was probably his only one. I peeked in the cabins, and there is no room for extras in those drawers."

"You'd be hopeless on a boat." Corrie laughed.

"Too true. That was sweet of Zeb to lend you his sweater." Adrianna shot her a sideways glance. Corrie folded her arms.

"Not this again. What do you want me to say?"

"Oh, nothing." Adrianna hummed a little. "Look, we're here. Make it quick, will you? Patrick is wondering where I am, I'm sure. I texted him ages ago. No cutesy goodbyes with the boys."

"Yes, mother."

Adrianna pulled into an empty parking spot and waved Corrie out of the car. Corrie strode as quickly as her short legs would go. It was cold without the sweater, but she'd be back in the warm car soon enough. It was nice of Zeb to lend her the sweater—the least she could do was return it promptly.

As she walked, Corrie reflected with satisfaction on their talk on the way home from the island. Zeb had finally spilled the secrets he'd been holding in so tightly. She felt they'd reached a new stage of trust and was excited about her next week on the boat.

The *Clicker* was docked near the end of the marina. Long before she reached the boat, she heard Jules laugh. She slowed and spied the *Clicker* through a sea of masts.

Corrie squinted, curious what the two were up to. Jules lounged on the bow deck with a beer in hand, chatting to Zeb, who wore nothing but his swimsuit. Corrie frowned. It was cold out now that the sun had vanished below the horizon. Why was Zeb in a swimsuit? Surely, he wasn't swimming at this hour.

Zeb walked around the side of the *Clicker*. He reached behind the life ring and pulled out a pair of small flippers. Corrie's curiosity intensified. Those weren't Zeb's scuba flippers. What was he doing?

With an ease born of much practice, Zeb slipped on his flippers. With no mask or wetsuit, he climbed to the top of the railing and balanced there for a moment. Then, with easy grace, he made a perfect dive into the water with hardly a splash.

Corrie's mouth fell open. Why on earth would Zeb dive into the frigid waters of the marina in the dark? There was nothing to see and nowhere to go. He wouldn't last more than a few minutes before succumbing to hypothermia.

But he had been entirely wet after the battle with Matt and Sucker and hadn't seemed to feel the cold at all.

And where was Zeb? He hadn't surfaced yet. He couldn't have swum that far. She scanned the waters of the marina, but there were no bubbles and no sign of Zeb.

Two minutes passed, then three. Corrie kept glancing at her watch. Jules sipped his beer and looked unconcerned. After five minutes, she wondered if she should tell Jules that Zeb was in the water. After seven minutes, she had just decided to alert him when Zeb's head surfaced. He hauled himself onto the dock, a fish in one hand.

"You got one," Jules called. "Excellent. There's a new recipe I want to try. Put it in the fridge for now."

Zeb disappeared into the cabin. Corrie shook her head, more confused than ever. Then she remembered that Adrianna was waiting for her, so she jogged to the *Clicker*.

Jules jumped when she called out his name.

"Corrie! You're back."

"I forgot to give Zeb his sweater," she said. "Here."

Jules leaned over the railing to grab it from her.

"Thanks," he said. "I'll give it to him. He's having a shower right now."

Corrie said her goodbyes and walked back along the dock. Had Zeb been underwater the whole time? She knew he was a free diver, but no one could hold their breath for seven minutes, surely. Was it even humanly possible?

A thought struck her. The enhancer that Miles spoke of, derived from the slime of the unicorn fish, was supposed to give people extra strength and speed underwater. What if it also helped with breath-holding? Was Zeb using the enhancer and not telling her? Jules was clearly in on the secret.

Corrie had thought they'd had a breakthrough, tonight, with Zeb telling her the truth of the sonar device, the creature names, and his mother's stories. But now, she wondered. Were those secrets only the tip of the iceberg?

PAULA

Scheduling was Paula's strength. Every one of Miles' appointments was meticulously recorded and planned on the calendar system. She noted the obvious things, of course, like time and place and person to meet, but also a suggested dress code and the tier of client—friend, contact, competition— which was a system Miles had devised and she had expanded. She didn't know what Miles would do without her, honestly. He would be a lost lamb, bleating to be led home. She was his shepherdess.

Paula amused herself with a vision of herself in a bonnet and holding a crook, then she banished the thought and turned to her work. She lifted her head at the sound of slow steps in the hallway.

Gavin and Flint, two Tangled Net employees, shuffled into her domain, the antechamber before Miles' office. She hid an expression of distaste. There was something slimy about Tangled Net. She'd heard enough over the past year of working for Miles to know what they did. While she understood the necessity of men like these in Miles' business, she didn't have to enjoy their company. They could do their job elsewhere and keep to themselves, as far as she was concerned.

Gavin was pale and walked with the help of a cane. It was so unlike him to show any weakness or emotion that Paula almost didn't recognize him. Flint was his usual blundering self.

"Is the boss in?" he rumbled. Paula stood up slowly, not wanting to appear as though she rushed for them.

"I'll see if he's available. One moment, please."

She sauntered to Miles' closed door, knocked gently, and entered at his reply.

"Tangled Net here to see you," she said softly when her head peeked through the doorway. "Do you have time before your one o'clock with Ms. White?"

"Yes, thanks, Paula." Miles smiled at her, although his face was drawn and worried. "I'll see them. You take such good care of me."

She smiled in return and walked back to the waiting men.

"Mr. Callahan will see you now," she said with a fake smile. She held the door open for the two men, and they shuffled past her. She closed the door with a solid click but immediately opened it a crack. It was a technique she'd practiced. It gave the impression that the door was closed but allowed her to hear meetings clearly. If anyone noticed the door open, she could claim that the latch was faulty. She stood beside the door and waited.

"We came for a debrief," said Gavin in a wheezy voice. "Here are all my notes from the horned fish mission. Everything should be there."

"I wish I could tell you to follow up on Zeballos Artino and his merry gang of do-gooders," said Miles in an aggrieved tone. "But my hands are tied. They somehow found out about certain—indiscretions—that would embarrass me if they should come to light. I'm afraid we'll have to shelve the mystery of the enhancer for now. Our next mission will be to plug the leaks. I thought we had covered our tracks, but apparently not well enough."

"If you give me the information, Tangled Net can follow up."

"Yes, I'll do that. That's all, gentlemen. Take it easy, Gavin. I want you in fine form, so take a few days off to recover."

"Yes, sir."

Paula slid back to her desk and was typing when Gavin and Flint left the office. They nodded at her and exited. Miles followed shortly after, adjusting a tie.

"I'm off to see Ms. White. Hold down the fort for me, will you?" He smiled at his own joke—Paula ran this ship, they both knew—and Paula chuckled.

"Of course, Mr. Callahan."

Paula gave Miles a few minutes to leave the building, then she picked up a random memo and walked purposefully into his office. It was the work of a moment to find the documents that Gavin had left. She flipped through them, her eyes widening at the contents.

So, Miles had found an opportunity that he couldn't take advantage of. Paula clicked her nails against the desk. He couldn't, but could she? She took the documents back to her desk and scanned each one, then saved them on her computer. Then she carefully took them back to Miles' desk.

Back in her chair, she flipped through her rolodex. She had business cards from every important person in the city that Miles had contact with. Her fingers paused at one, and she picked up the phone.

"Please leave a message for Ryan Stokes. This is Paula Rossi, Miles Callahan's personal assistant. I have some information Mr. Stokes will be interested in. Please set up a confidential meeting."

ZEBALLOS

Zeb woke early. The sun hadn't yet broken the horizon, but he felt wide awake. The aches from yesterday had subsided, although he knew that they would feel even better in the water. There was nothing more refreshing than a swim in the early morning, unless it was a little music from his whistle, made from the rib bone of a callo and given to him by his mother many years ago.

It didn't take much for Zeb to convince himself. He slipped into his swimsuit, grabbed his whistle from a drawer, then left his cabin. He left a note in the galley for Jules—not that Jules would be up before Zeb came back, but Zeb had learned his lesson about the importance of notes—and moved to the deck. Gentle waves lapped against the hull.

Zeb took a deep breath and stretched his arms above his head. The pre-dawn air was pleasantly cool on his bare skin. No one was up at such an early hour, and he had the marina to himself. Only the soft clinking of halyards on sailboat masts disturbed the hush.

Zeb slipped on his flippers and dived into the calm water. It was as refreshing as he had hoped. He pointed his arms in front of him with the whistle in his hands and undulated his body in swift motions to swim out of the marina and past the breakwater. He rolled in a corkscrew motion, just for fun. He swam deeper, and a harbor seal rose from the depths to investigate. Its whiskered face was so inquisitive and comical that Zeb released a bubble of laughter. The seal shied away, but Zeb called it back with a few clicks of apology.

The seal swam beside him for a while, each enjoying the other's company. Zeb corkscrewed again, and the seal copied him. Zeb beamed. This was living. The seal finally lost interest when Zeb rose toward the surface for air, and it swam back the way they had traveled.

The surface was near. It glistened like an ever-moving mirror, mesmerizing in its beauty. Zeb sped up. It had been a while since he'd tried breaching, but he was stronger now. There was no one around at this hour, and it was too tempting to deny himself the fun. He threw himself upward in a rush of speed.

Zeb burst from the surface until only his knees and feet remained submerged. He crashed into the sea with a tremendous splash. Bubbles of laughter escaped him, and he bobbed to the surface for more air.

When his chuckles finally subsided, he aimed his body toward a tiny outcrop of land, no more than a rock for birds to sit on. Zeb climbed gingerly up and perched on a flat rock. Bringing the callo whistle to his lips, he began to play.

It was a haunting, melancholic call, sounding less like an instrument than the sighing of wind or the calls of a whale. The music soothed Zeb and put him in a contemplative mood. He felt so happy to be free—of Miles and his goons, of that tank on the island, of his lies to Corrie—that he had to express his joy somehow. Swimming and playing his whistle fit the bill.

He didn't play for long. When a fish jumped in the distance, Zeb stopped his music. The fish were always lively at dawn. He felt like chasing a few, for fun. They never knew what to think of him.

He dived in again and a thought struck him. What if he made the noise of the sonar device again? He could produce it himself, now, with no need for the boat. He wondered if there were any creatures nearby. His rising excitement told him to find out.

It took a little trying to find the right frequency. When he had it, he hummed deep in his chest every few seconds, just like the device. It worked at the boat, so it might work here. He somersaulted in the water to release his feelings. Would he see the usual strolias today, or something else? Maybe the ligan would visit, or a kroll. He hoped something was near. He still didn't know how to find answers to his questions about the fish, but the more he knew, the better. Maybe he could even understand what his questions were, given enough sightings. What did he truly want? At the heart of it, Zeb wanted to understand where his mother had come from, and to understand why he was different.

The currents on his skin alerted him to a presence, different from the perch swimming overhead. It was large—not nearly as large as the ligan, but almost as large as Zeb—and swimming parallel to him. He couldn't quite tell what it was. It swam like a seal but wasn't rotund enough. His curiosity was piqued, and he aimed his body in the presence's direction, continuing to make the sound every few seconds.

When he was close enough to see through the green water, he strained his eyes in the right direction. There was a flash of white, then he lost sight again. What was white under the water? Zeb wracked his brain, thinking of all the local fish he knew then remembering the tales of his mother. Nothing white sprang to mind. He put on a burst of speed to catch up to the presence.

He closed his eyes and let his other senses take over. The presence was out of sight, but not out of sensing. It was slender and undulated with a familiar swimming action. What did it remind Zeb of?

When it came to him, he almost stopped in shock. It reminded him of what he must look like swimming underwater, with his arms forward in a point, and his head making a small disturbance in the plane of his undulating body.

Zeb burst into a frenzy of motion to catch up. He had to know. Who was swimming in the middle of the channel? Was there a boat nearby? The figure had no tanks or mask, he was certain. Was it another free diver?

He approached the figure, which suddenly stopped. Zeb's heart raced with excitement, then he checked himself. How would he explain his own presence, with no wetsuit so far from land?

He didn't care. This person, whoever they were, clearly had similar habits. They might be understanding of his strange customs. He swam closer, until he could see the white again.

Zeb stopped. There was a woman under the water, a woman with hair as white-blond as his own, and skin as pale as his mother's had been. She floated in midwater, graceful and ethereal, her hair drifting in the currents. Her pale eyes, so like his own in the mirror, gazed at him without expression. She was dressed in gauzy coverings the color of kelp that drifted like seaweed around her slender form. Her feet were strange, unnaturally elongated, with webbing between the toes.

Zeb almost choked. She was a younger version of his mother, come to life. There was no wetsuit and no rushing to the surface to breathe. She floated easily, raking her expressionless eyes over his body and face. Zeb reached out with both hands in a yearning gesture. He didn't know what he was trying to do—maybe touch her to see if she was real?

As if he had broken a spell, the woman twisted with dangerous speed and dived away from him with her coverings flowing behind. Zeb let out a crying bubble of despair and plunged after her. This was what he had been searching for. He needed to find her. He needed to talk to her, ask her questions, know who she was, what she was. He needed her.

She was out of sight before Zeb started moving. He closed his eyes and pursued her using his other senses. She was quick, much quicker than he. Zeb felt her move farther and farther away until she was at the edge of his limits of detection. He strained his senses, willing them to spread farther than ever, and he pumped his body until his muscles screamed.

Eventually, he stopped. His heart pounded, and his lungs burned with the need for air. Tears leaked from his eyes to join the saltiness of the sea.

How could he come so close, and still know nothing?

Continue the adventure in *Surfacing*, book three of the Nautilus Legends...

When Zeb discovers someone attracting mysterious creatures for nefarious purposes, can he and Corrie uncover the truth before the world of the creatures is exposed?

Find *Surfacing* at your favorite online retailer today!

www.emmashelford.com/nautilus-legends.html

Want to stay in touch? Subscribe to my newsletter, in which you'll receive a free ebook, news about new releases, cover reveals, and giveaways exclusive to the newsletter. Be the first to know!

www.emmashelford.com/signup.html

Want to stay in touch on Facebook instead? Join Emma Shelford's Fantastical Lair, where we share our book reviews and our love of all things fantasy.

www.facebook.com/groups/fantasticallair

If you have a moment, I would love a review on your favorite retailer (see www.emmashelford.com/nautilus-legends.html for links). It's a wonderful way to support an author, as reviews makes a huge difference for a book's visibility. I whole-heartedly appreciate every single review!

Emma Shelford

ALSO BY EMMA SHELFORD

<u>Nautilus Legends</u>
Free Dive
Caught
Surfacing
More to come

<u>Musings of Merlin Series</u>
Ignition
Winded
Floodgates
Buried
More to come

<u>Breenan Series</u>
Mark of the Breenan
Garden of Last Hope
Realm of the Forgotten

ACKNOWLEDGEMENTS

Thank you to my editors, new and old, who polished the story to a shine: Gillian Brownlee, Wendy and Chris Callendar, and Brianna Wright. Christien Gilston produced another thrilling cover. Dr. Erin Langwith and Dr. Caitlin Wright kindly provided veterinarian advice, and Dr. Danielle Winget checked the science (any fabrications are my own). Many thanks to Clare Hollocks for naming inspiration.

ABOUT THE AUTHOR

Emma Shelford loves the ocean and fantasy and has now brought the two together through the Nautilus Legends. She spends as much time as she can on the ocean, and David Attenborough's Blue Planet is a perennial thrill for her.

www.ingramcontent.com/pod-product-compliance
Lightning Source LLC
Chambersburg PA
CBHW021321190726
48288CB00003B/912